TRAIN, TRACKS AND TALES

AN ANTHOLOGY OF TRAIN NARRATIVES

BIBIN SEBASTIAN | GEORGE SEBASTIAN

Copyright © Bibin Sebastian, George Sebastian
All Rights Reserved.

This book has been self-published with all reasonable efforts taken to make the material error-free by the author. No part of this book shall be used, reproduced in any manner whatsoever without written permission from the author, except in the case of brief quotations embodied in critical articles and reviews.

The Author of this book is solely responsible and liable for its content including but not limited to the views, representations, descriptions, statements, information, opinions and references ["Content"]. The Content of this book shall not constitute or be construed or deemed to reflect the opinion or expression of the Publisher or Editor. Neither the Publisher nor Editor endorse or approve the Content of this book or guarantee the reliability, accuracy or completeness of the Content published herein and do not make any representations or warranties of any kind, express or implied, including but not limited to the implied warranties of merchantability, fitness for a particular purpose. The Publisher and Editor shall not be liable whatsoever for any errors, omissions, whether such errors or omissions result from negligence, accident, or any other cause or claims for loss or damages of any kind, including without limitation, indirect or consequential loss or damage arising out of use, inability to use, or about the reliability, accuracy or sufficiency of the information contained in this book.

Made with ♥ on the Notion Press Platform
www.notionpress.com

Contents

Contents

Foreword

In an era where movement and connection define much of our existence, the allure of train narratives remains undiminished. Trains, with their rhythmic clatter and endless tracks, have long captured the imagination of storytellers and readers alike. They serve as powerful symbols of journey and transformation, evoking a sense of adventure, romance, and sometimes, mystery.

"Train, Tracks and Tales: An Anthology of Train Narratives" delves into the multifaceted world of trains, exploring their historical and cultural significance, their role as connectors and separators, and their place in social and political narratives. This anthology brings together a collection of short stories, personal essays, and poems that celebrate the essence of train travel and its impact on our lives.

The contributors to this anthology have crafted pieces that reflect personal journeys, historical events, and societal shifts, offering readers a rich tapestry of experiences and insights. Through their words, we traverse landscapes both familiar and foreign, witnessing transformations and exploring the depths of human connection.

As you embark on this literary journey, allow yourself to be transported by the stories and poems within these pages. Let the rhythmic motion of the train guide you through tales of adventure, romance, and introspection. "Train, Tracks and Tales" is more than just an anthology; it is an exploration of the human experience through the lens of one of the most enduring symbols of travel.

Enjoy the ride.

Bibin Sebastian , George Sebastian

Acknowledgements

- **Dr. Santulan Mahanta**, Assistant Professor at H. P. B. Girls' College since 2016, specializes in railway research. With an M. Phil. and Ph.D. in English (Linguistics and Phonetics) from the English and Foreign Languages University, he is known for his work on Indian Railways. His efforts have earned him recognition as a renowned railway historian. Recently, he published "Rail Puran" in Assamese, pioneering railway literature in Indian languages.
- **Keerthy Elza Tes Mathew** is an Assistant Professor in the Department of English at Marian College, Kuttikkanam (Autonomous) with 8 years of teaching experience. Her areas of interest include Film Studies and Cultural Studies, where she actively engages in academic exploration and research.
- **Swayama Sengupta**, a doctoral scholar at Amity University Kolkata, is a double gold medalist from Adamas University. Passionate about heritage, she admires Ray and Austen. Currently, she is studying Japanese at NILI, Kolkata, and composing Bengali rhymes to stay awake during train rides and traffic.
- **Dr. Richa Biswal**, an Assistant Professor of English at Maharaja Purna Chandra Autonomous College, Odisha, specializes in Indian Poetics, John Donne, Comparative Literature, Twentieth Century British Literature, and Postcolonialism. She holds a Ph.D. from the University of Allahabad. Fluent in multiple languages, she has authored two critical books, 25 book chapters, and numerous journal papers. She is a member of several academic societies and has presented at numerous seminars and conferences.
- **Arnab Chatterjee** is an avid collector of selves. He lives in a town called Berhampore while portraying his writings with the sublime aesthetics of pastoral Bengal, and the voices lost in

Modernity. He hopes to publish all his writings, if he can stop reading others' works more. He took up many hobbies which are constantly getting tarnished by academics, but he still tries to keep up with everything while hoping to find himself. He is published nationally and internationally.

- **Smeha John Machado** is an Assistant Professor of English at Kamaraj College, Thoothukudi. Passionate about literature, she is an avid reader who dreams of becoming an author. Despite challenges, she cleared the National Eligibility Test on her first attempt and has numerous publications. She is committed to inspiring her students and continuously learning new languages. With a love for both realism and surrealism in literature, she tirelessly pursues her passion for creating art.

- **Sakshi Nain Bishnoi** (she/they) has completed her masters in English Literature from The English and Foreign Languages University, Hyderabad (2021-23). The politics of migration and gender is intertwined in Sakshi's lived experience and she has chosen to emulsify theory and her praxis and work on the same as well. Sakshi is keenly interested in the interface of migration, education, literature and gender and is currently translating feminist texts in their native tongue, in order to make the texts more accessible to the gender minorities in her village and nearby areas.

- **Nikitha Nelson** is an English Language and Literature student, pursuing her Masters from Mar Ivanios College, Thiruvananthapuram. Writing is a passionate endeavour for her and she has always been ardent in honing her writing skills. She challenges herself by enrolling in various literary activities, including publishing and book clubs. She is attentive to public welfare and prioritizes writing about social issues and mental health. Life as an academic and an instructor is what she aims for and this inspires her to participate in conferences and paper presentations. Her first poetry collection came out in March 2024, titled "Red Roses on a Wreath".

- **Itrat Khan,** a PhD scholar, writer, and poet, has made significant contributions to the fields of postcolonialism, cultural studies, and power-knowledge relations. Her extensive research papers delve into the complexities of these areas, shedding light on the intricate dynamics between colonial legacies, cultural identities, and the dissemination of knowledge.

- **Devika Vinod** is a Ph.D. JRF Research Scholar at the Research and PG Department of English, St. Thomas College (Autonomous), Thrissur, Kerala, affiliated to the University of Calicut. She works on postcolonial migration and diaspora for her research. She is also interested in gender studies, memory studies and existentialism.

- **Rahul Bajpai**, a PhD scholar at the University of Lucknow, is researching heroic narratives in translation. His academic journey began in his hometown, where he excelled in studies and developed a passion for storytelling. His research focuses on literature, identity, and folklore, emphasizing cultural identity in narrative form. An aspiring writer, Rahul is dedicated to expanding his literary knowledge and aims to contribute meaningfully to the field through his research and creative writings.

- **Ligia Nazareth** is an English Lecturer at Don Bosco College, Kottiyam, Kollam. She is a passionate teacher who inspires her learners to pursue their goals. She is an ardent speaker, Quotes' writer and a bibliophile. She hails from the coastal town of Thangassery, which is historically and socially significant. She is actively involved in various Green initiatives and academic activities.

- **Dr.Beena Anil** works as Associate Professor at the Department of English, Shrimathi Devkunvar Nanalal Bhatt Vaishnav College for Women, Chennai. She is a writer and authored 4 books as well as published 25 research papers in various national and international journals of repute.

- **Sonika Sheoran**, a Ph.D. student in film studies at Chandigarh University, is deeply dedicated and passionate about cinematic arts and storytelling. She earned her master's in English

Literature from Panjab University in 2020, honing her analytical and critical thinking skills. Her background in literature enriches her current research in film studies. Beyond academics, Sonika is multifaceted and creative, drawing inspiration from diverse perspectives through extensive reading, which enhances her narrative understanding and film analysis.

- **Leena P.** is a cinephile who loves traveling by train across India. She holds a master's degree in English and a Higher Diploma in Software Engineering. With over 14 years of experience in software programming and HR development, Leena was also an RJ with AIR Chennai B Youth English for 4 years. A prize-winning blogger and finalist in 'Super Mom 2008,' she is an active member of The Malayalee Club's Literary and Cultural wing. Recently, she read her poem 'Medicine to my pain' to a packed audience and was involved in the pre-production and shooting of the Tamil movie 'Soppana Sundari.' Born and raised in Chennai, she resides in Mylapore with her family.

- **Ardra Ann Thomas** is a Research Scholar in the Department of English at St Thomas College, Palai. She is a JRF fellowship holder, and her academic journey is marked by a deep investment in exploring the myriad nuances of English. Her research focuses on Postmodernism, Posthumanism and Media Studies. She has presented papers at International Seminars and Conferences. She harbours an inexplicable love for the language and is deeply invested in exploring the nuances of English in every way possible.

- **Himanshu Kumar** is a poet and translator who migrated from the City of Nawabs to the City of Djinns, where he has been teaching undergraduate and postgraduate students for more than a decade. His literary endeavours give him pleasure although he can't claim the same for all his readers. He is currently looking at you while you are trying to find the most suitable adjective to appreciate his work.

- **Suparna Roy**, an Assistant Professor of English at the Global Institute of Management and Technology, is an independent researcher with a Master's in English Literature (2020) and a B.Ed. (2022). She has over three years of teaching experience and 20+ publications. Her research focuses on South Asian studies, Gender, and Literature. Selected for the 2022 Summer Sexuality Fellowship at the California Institute of Integral Studies, she completed a project on Queer Identities and Gender Intersectionality under Think India.

- **Reema Sara Benson** is a second-year degree student at Marian College, Kuttikkanam, hailing from Aluva. An avid reader and passionate storyteller, she enjoys weaving tales and engaging in public speaking. Reema's multifaceted personality shines through her love for simple pleasures and her dedication to various pursuits. Whether she's baking stories or captivating an audience, Reema brings enthusiasm and creativity to everything she does.

- **Dr. Sujarani Mathew**, an Associate Professor of English at Kuriakose Elias College Mannanam (affiliated with Mahatma Gandhi University, Kerala), holds academic credentials from the Central Universities of Hyderabad and Pondicherry. She has authored numerous articles in reputed national and international journals and academic books on topics like Gender Studies, Neurolinguistics, and Informatics. Additionally, she wrote a short story collection titled "Teen Vibes." Sujarani Mathew is listed in the website- womenwritersofkerala.com. She resides at a scenic spot in the suburbs of Marangattupilly, with her husband and her two boys and spends her free time watching their frisky goats and mulling over the web of life.

- **Durdanah Masoodi** holds a Master of Arts in Political Science from Jamia Millia Islamia and a Bachelor of Arts in Political Science from Miranda House, University of Delhi. She has qualified for UGC-NET/JRF and has published several articles and book reviews in reputed journals. Her research focuses on contemporary political issues and social dynamics, including gender studies and public health crises in Kashmir

- **Dr. Niborna Hazarika** has recently completed her Ph.D. at the

Centre for English Studies, Jawaharlal Nehru University. She had also completed her MPhil from the same center. During her doctoral study, she was awarded the prestigious ICSSR Institutional Doctoral Fellowship, and the institute she was affiliated with was the Centre for the Study of Developing Societies (CSDS). Her research interests include regional studies, postcolonial studies as well as travel writing. She has published several papers till now in various reputed journals and has presented papers at sixteen national and international conferences till now. Currently, she is associated with a project titled 'Anuvadini' under the Ministry of Education, Govt. of India.

- **Namrata Mukherjee**, born and raised in Kolkata, is a writer, reader, and lifelong bibliophile. An English literature fellow, her world brims with stories, adventures, and journeys. With a lifelong passion for books, her list of favorite authors includes Ruskin Bond, Cecelia Ahern, JD Salinger, Neil Gaiman, and Charlotte Brontë. Namrata has a rich history as an educator and currently works with language models, expanding her horizon as an author. Her widely published and awarded poems reflect her literary prowess.

- **Dr. K. Venkata Lakshmi** is a Professor of English and Dean of the Department at KPRIT. She has attended 5 FDPs and 5 ELTAI webinars, and published 3 papers in international conferences and workshops. She has also participated in 2 NIPAM awareness programs and 7 national workshops, and earned 2 NPTEL certifications. Additionally, she has experience as a paper setter for VBIT and has served as a BOS Member and subject expert for 3 years at Nawab Shah Alam Khan College of Engineering and Technology.

- **Kavya Dinesh**, a literary enthusiast and budding writer, holds a Master's in English Language and Literature from the University of Kerala. She served as an Assistant Professor at Gregorian College, guiding students in psychoanalytical studies. She co-authored poetry anthologies and is currently pursuing a

Bachelor of English Education. Her interests include detective and psychological thrillers and ecocritical narratives. She stays updated on advancements in communication and technology, incorporating them into her teaching. She is forever a learner.

- **Disha Shetty** is a student at Garden City University, Bangalore, pursuing a Master's in English Literature with a specialization in Computational Linguistics. She loves writing and exploring the intersection of technology and literature for the betterment of humanity. Her passion for creating and identifying gaps in her fields of interest is one of her best qualities. A favorite line from her writing is: "I burn like ice and melt like fire, neither I have a name nor a desire."

- **Neenu Kuruvilla**, currently a research scholar at Mercy College, Palakkad, affiliated with the University of Calicut, focuses on body-soul binaries, challenging religious norms by emphasizing bodily desires. She also works part-time at All India Radio, Kochi. With a keen interest in mythology and archetypes, she aims to merge aesthetics and philosophy with everyday reality, making arts and literature more beneficial to humanity.

- **Preeti Sharma**, a Ph.D. candidate at Amity University, Noida, India, has her research interest in religion, feminism, entertainment, and lost culture and traditions. Her academic pursuits are driven by a fervent dedication to preserving cultural heritage and unraveling the intricate societal dynamics at play. Through her research, she navigates the intersections of these diverse fields, uncovering connections and insights that illuminate the complexities of human experience.

- **Vastav Shastri** from Surat, Gujarat, holds a B.A. and M.A. in English Literature from Veer Narmad South Gujarat University. An Assistant Professor at SDJ International College, Vesu, he teaches Business Communication to B.B.A and M.B.A. students. He is pursuing a Ph.D. in English and has been in education since 2015. Additionally, he is a rail enthusiast and holds a Diploma and Certificate in Travel and Tourism with distinction.

- **Inderjot Kaur**, an avid traveler and passionate writer, seeks inspiration worldwide, embracing mystery, adventure, and discovery. Her journeys, from misty mountains to bustling cities, fuel her creativity and shape her into a versatile wordsmith. Through her storytelling, Inderjot invites others to join her exhilarating journeys, sharing tales of exploration and the beauty of the human experience.
- **Aardra H**, residing in Sasthamcotta, Kollam, is a literary enthusiast, nature lover, and infrequent writer. She graduated from Sree Narayana College, Kollam, and completed her post-graduation at S N College for Women, Kollam. With a strong academic background in English Language and Literature, Aardra has published research articles in various journals. She currently works as an Assistant Professor (on contract) in the Department of English at Sree Narayana College, Kollam, Kerala.

CHAPTER ONE

Derailed Memories

Santulan Mahanta

As Nairatmya opened his hard disk and scrolled through the folder of 2012, his eyes got fixed on a thumbnail. All this afternoon he was in a constant irritation. Irritation with being stuck in the job and not taking a trip without a destination. The job is taking a toll on his mind, body, and hobby. But he can contribute to the society better than he could with his hobby. He can teach, and he can pay taxes for a better society. His hobby doesn't. His reputation, as a railway photographer, however, earned him some respect which he could not hold for long. And his reputation as a teacher earned him a position he could not afford to let go of. All he can do now is scour through a hundred thousand photographs he took a decade ago and share them every once in a while. Sometimes all these digital photographs just feel like digital garbage where he happens to ragpick. As of now, that is what his hobby has been reduced to. Scouting through the railway tracks and clicking the life around the railways is no longer an option for a teacher. In a small township like this, he may not know everyone, but everyone knows him. So holding a camera and taking a photographing stance by the tracksides would call for so many explanations that he should rather not think about it at all.

When you are a teacher, you can have some decent hobbies, hobbies which people must understand. Photographing random things and random people by the railway tracks is not one of them. It's as much unacceptable like trying date with your student. Plant a tree, orchestrate a street play, sit at a tea stall and sip a hot cup of tea in between occasional puffs, sing a wierd song at the farewell parties, spend some time and money at a bar, or even wear a skinfit t-shirt. You are acceptable. However, you can go away on a photographing retreat and take random pictures of the same subjects, and share them later with people – now that is somewhat acceptable. However, the job does not permit a leave of absence for such retreats. When you enter academia, it is a full-time job, you sleep on taxed times on taxpayer's money. Your vacation is a paid-up vacation, so that you can be available anytime anywhere, and be prepared for the classes when it is over. It pays well, and you can pay well for the stress-induced illnesses as well. Everything in the cosmos is thus perfectly balanced. Then it is perhaps the age which restricts him from doing stuff like walking from one end to the other end of the longest railway bridge in Vembanad. He cannot do such adventures anymore. That was a different time, a different age. So every now and then Nairtmya can do only one thing, going through the old stuff, sharing it with the virtual world – feeling sad about not being able to do that stuff anymore, and feeling elated with every like and comment that post garners. Today this was another photograph that would need an accompanying story as a caption.

It was a different world and a different summer afternoon. By then he had a new hobby. Photographing the life around the railway. Experimenting with both the camera set-up and perspectives of railways. Nairatmya novicely felt that he had attained perfection in photographing the trains and locomotives from every possible angle. Now it was time for something new. Something from the railways though. Just the platforms and the tracks and the rolling stocks don't make the railway. For a passenger that was everything that makes a railway, for a railway enthusiast that was just the solar system in the railway universe. There were galaxies to explore, fathom the unfathomed depths of railway yards, railway workshops, and railway colonies which hold much more mysteries. Looking for subjects he'd scout the tracks through Lucknow. Heisenberg could point to himn for his illustration of uncertainty principle. If that city with ten stations was a molecule, he was a restless electron moving on the marked orbits of railway tracks. He knew every fastener of every sleeper on the railway tracks. What he sought, however, were things existing and things happening by the tracksides. Things that Nairatmya visualised were beyond the capacity of his point-and-shoot camera. What he aspired to was the perfection level of railway photography set by Apurva Bahadur, Nandakumar Narasimhan, Lalam Mandavkar, etc. Their photographs had untold stories that were never told. But a DSLR was neither within his budget nor his skillsets. Yet he took it as a learning stage with camera optics and pushed his camera to its limits. He wished his physics education didn't end at twelfth standard. But not all the photographers were students of science. They experimented, and they learnt. For such experiments, you need some solitariness, away from the prying eyes of the crowds. And there was this spot where he could get absolute solitude.

That afternoon he reached the foot overbridge that connects Alambagh Workshop and Lucknow Junction Coaching Depot. It was seldom used by the railway workers for whom it was set there. Lines exiting from Lucknow Charbagh station bifurcates just there to move towards Kanpur Central and Moradabad respectively. Towards the east, one can get a view of the twin stations of Charbagh and Lucknow Junction. The former belongs to the Northern Railway and the latter to the North Eastern Railway. These two stations have their own definitions of cleanliness and orderliness. But from where he was standing, these were not visible. The only thing he could see at that moment was the shade of red cast by the setting sun on both the majestic buildings. They were shining quite bright and the hue was changing from golden to red and then to crimson. He wondered how it would look like from the sky when these evening hues cast the colours of Holi on the majestic Charbagh station building that was built like the board of chess. It is one of the most majestic station buildings culminating the Indo-Persian and Rajput architecture. Kanpur Central wanted to imitate that style but did not succeed. Awadh had the money, resources, and the importance all along. Charbagh, at that time of the day, from that spot, appeared really surreal. That is a view one cannot get from the platforms, nor from the trains. Being a novice, he tried to capture that. But some things are meant for the eyes only, not for the lenses. One can ignore the electric catenaries in the mental picture, but not without the software in a digital photograph. This thing did disappoint him that day. But not now, after more than a decade. Now he understands that this mental picture that he carries within him is just his own intellectual private possession, it was his sole experience trekking the tracks to reach that spot. And that itself is the achievement, the prize of a treasure hunt.

Nairatmya shut down his camera and leaned against the railings of the foot overbridge. He was still facing the east, still his eyes fixed on the marvelous structures. Two electric locomotives were parked to his left. One would take charge of the Delhi-bound Vaishali Express when it arrives with a diesel locomotive and undergoes a reversal at Lucknow junction. The other one would take charge of the Kaifiyat Express – the train named after renowned poet Kaifi Azmi. He always found Vaishali Express more appealing, perhaps due to its relation to Buddha in ancient history. A trackman was doing his last beat of the day on the mainline of the down yard. His work hours would end in another one and a half hours. His orange shirt was stuck to his back, drenched with the sweat of his hard toil. Had Camus seen this trackman, would he have chosen the myth of Sysiphus as a metaphore to modern man's existence? This trackman is that modern Sysiphus than any other man. Every day he toils the same way that he had the previous day and his job is never done.

The man moved away to a safe distance from the tracks as he heard the honking of an approaching train. No one knows who would spit from the moving train or throw some garbage. Often those things land on these fellows. Ganga-Sutlej Express to Dhanbad was approaching with a Ludhiana-based WDM2 locomotive. "That's a hell of a locoshed. They decided to remain conventional and refused to accept any new generation locomotive. That's typical of Punjabi. They love their machines raw and rugged, not complicated and crippled with microchip controls. There is a rare chance of failure of Ludhiana's locomotives." Nairatmya thought. As the train train tried to gain momentum from momentary slowing down, the ALCo locomotive belched out a clog of smoke and started chugging heavily. These locomotives were more humane than the new generation General Motors locomotives. New locomotives lack that humane touch. One could just listen to the chugging and know when the locomotive was trying to churn out more power from its V16 engine. For sixty years they have faithfully served the Indian Railways, a feat unparalleled anywhere in the world and yet went heavily unnoticed. These locomotives became the platform for not only later generations of diesel locomotives but also for several electric locomotive classes. And here was one in the near original raw form passing by. The other day a friend from the United States asked him where in India he could travel behind an ALCo locomotive end to end in a journey. At sixty, one retires from the job. The ALCo were also on the verge of retirement. Nairatmya always admired these machines.

Afternoon times in Lucknow were full of actions. Lohith Express should have arrived from the opposite direction. Lohit Express slot is shared with Himgiri Express on three days and three Amarnath Expresses on rest of the three days of the week. Then there would be Up Amritsar Mail, that train which had a disaster in 1930s at a speed of 100kmph, and our fastest trains still boast of just sixty kilometre speed increment another 80 years since then. Then it'd be the Singrauli bound Triveni Express, a portion of which would go to Shaktinagar. As soon as it departs Dehradun bound Janata Express would occupy the pkatform. Quite rush hour it was. Messing up of one train would mean loss of punctuality of all the others that follow. But after that almost for an hour Platform 1 would be free until Avadh Assam Express arrives. Gandhidham Express would be put on either Platform 7 or 6. Once Jhansi Intercity departs, platform 7 would be free. Again after Gandhidham that platform would have a breather till the Begampura Express arrives from Varanasi. That was another rockstar train. Nairatmya had wonderful experience of journey by that train. In a single line route it was doing 120kmph hauled by an ageing ALCo from Ludhiana. A thirty year old machine still delivering its maximum is a common thing in the railways, but an unthinkable feat if it was the roadways. Platform 1 would be occupied again by Guwahati-bound Rajdhani Express via Varanasi. This Rajdhani is a shame to the entire Rajdhani category. It does not take the shortest route, neither is this one a fast one. On the timetable, it is slower than the Poorvottar Sampark Kranti Express. This one is an appeasement to the Khagaria vote bank, not to serve northeastern India. Tughlakabad even failed to provide a good locomotive on several occasions and such a prestigious train could be seen running with a freight locomotive. All the while one could hear the busy commotions and bustles at the station. But to the outside traffic on the road the platforms appeared as silent like an examination hall.

Nairatmya just imagined the amount of work pressure station master Nitin must have felt. There were many other trains which he didn't remember at that moment. All these would occupy different platforms, but arrive and depart by the same tracks. Order of preference of the trains is something the section controllers find nightmarish. As a passenger a delayed train means all the rage targeted on the drivers. But the poor fellows have nothing to do. Section controllers decide which train to be moved and when. For busy sections like Allahabad-Kanpur where the train number exceeds twice the capacity of the lines, those poor controllers must feel like committing suicide before suffering a panic attack . Not everyone can handle such a traffic. These are some of the best men working the worst section of Indian Railways. For Nairatmya, railway is a fascinating subject which is unattractive to work in. Yet he applied for railway jobs twice but didn't bother to check the results. He would rather write about railways like Ruskin Bond than be a part of it.

Just then a man arrived there, holding his two-year-old son in his arms. Seeing Nairatmya there he gave a friendly smile. He went to the other end of the overbridge facing Lucknow Junction Coaching Depot and stood there. The rake of Pushpak Express was still getting readied there. It was thoroughly washed, carriage undergears checked, and brake power certificate already issued for its almost one and half thousand kilometres journey to Mumbai. There was the rake of Lucknow-Chandigarh Express in the pit line too. It was the North Eastern Railway depot, but all the shunting work was being done by a Northern Railway's Lucknow shed's diesel locomotive. Nairatmya had met him a couple of weeks before. They didn't exchange names but Nairatmya's camera didn't bother that man either. He works in Alambagh Railway Workshop, and spends the day making the coaches rolling worthy. No amount of machine presence can lessen the burden on these people. Of course, some works need traditional human muscles and skills rather than machine powers. And then there are some works that prefer the traditional way and resist much change in the workspace environment. Sometimes traditions appear like a barrier to changes, be it the workspace or our family space, or even the unavoidable social space.

Tradition. That's a heavy word with multiple layers of understanding and action. Sometimes it is regressive and some other times it is just paying respect to the past. Alambagh workshop is one of the oldest workshops in the Indian railways. Somewhere has the tradition kept it from changing? A torrent of sudden discourses flash flooded his mind. Perhaps he is wrong in understanding tradition and heritage that way. Or perhaps he is not always. Who decides these rights and wrongs? Every tradition has a traceable beginning in history when it was considered as a new school of thought. What happens when modernity meets tradition? The rise of the railways changed the entire tradition of pilgrimage in India. Tradition too had a change of its tradition. Earlier people used to go on perilous pilgrimage when they could afford some time during the farming. Railways reduced the travel times to a journey of a mere couple of days instead of months in traditional travelling. So pilgrimage became easier, pilgrim places soon started flooding with people all around the year instead of any particular season. Our traditions changed when a modern thing called the railway arrived. It's really hard to get the meaning of tradition, to get what constitutes tradition. Tradition itself changes sometimes. Churchil once said, "we shape our buildings; thereafter they shape us." That holds good for tradition as well. It's just a matter and point of time when we shape a tradition.

That locomotive now shunted a readied rake and then came to stand light straight in front of the father and son duo. It had a name – Prabal. Prabal, meaning powerful in Hindi. What a name for this relentless metal worker! The father was telling something to his son pointing to Prabal. Nairatmya couldn't hear that. Perhaps he was saying that during the day the father builds those coaches, repairs them, and then after the wash they roll away for far-off places. The boy cannot understand the departmental procedures, so that must be the way the father would have told him. The little boy doesn't know anything about the trains, except his fascination for the long metal snake like many others of his age. The very sight of the train makes the children of that age look with their eyes wide open with awe. For them, there are very few wonders in the world and a train comes at the first place. Now just imagine your father telling you that he works on that wonder of the world and how would your reaction be? Perhaps that little boy had had the same kind of thoughts and feelings at that moment. Nairatmya too had a flashback from his childhood.

He was in the kindergarten in a remote corner of Assam. One evening after returning from college, his father took him to the railway station. Their town had two stations, one is popularly known as JPR, from the erstwhile Jorhat Provincial Railway and the other one was just Jorhat Town. Their home was just across the river near JPR. They reached the JPR where a steam locomotive was waiting for clearance with a passenger train. Apart from seeing a steam engine in pictures, this was his first encounter with one in real life. He saw a fireman shoving some coal in quick succession. His father told him that the smoke now would be black at first and then it'd be somewhat of a copper tint when the coal gets burnt properly. The cab of the engine had some number which he doesn't remember now. All he remembers is the peeling coats of paint over that. Apart from that the engine did look quite old and weary. It was not a perfect black beauty, but rather a fading ghost from the past. But he was quite excited to have seen a steam engine from such close. He wondered how can water move a train. He thought he'd know everything about a steam engine like his father when he grew up. What he didn't know was that it was only a couple of years before the steam engines went away. He would never get to know the steam engines. That afternoon Nairtmya kept staring at the engine, and so did his father for a long time. Then his father said to the engine, "Should it happen to you like this, leaking water?" Nairtmya couldn't understand anything, but he could sense the sadness in his father's voice.

There was a time when his father's generation saw those engines working superfast trains, they travelled behind those engines and travelled the entire country on steam-hauled trains. Those were the normal, usual things back then. He saw his father's painting of a steam engine, the deflector on it had the name 'Shaktishel' just like that diesel locomotive had its name Prabal. He still recalls the number of Shaktishel – 2112. Twenty years since then Nairatmya saw the skeletal remains of a steam engine at New Jalpaiguri yard while going home in Assam. On his return trip to Lucknow, he just got off there and went for a close inspection. He felt a shivering of joy, looking at the road number amidst that debris which still was shining – 2112. Shaktishel after all these years. Shaktishel or the power-stuff, the mythological spear that killed Laxman in Ramayana. The same name was given to the alive engine of this debris. There was a time it was working, moving, puffing like a human being.

There were many like Shaktishel. Babrubahana, Chandika, Chitrangada, Hidimba, Pawan-Nandan, Menaka, Urvashi, Chaitali, Jatrik, Jahnavi – all these were names of some steam engines he heard from his father. How come they have these names? His father had a logbook of all those engines – their names, their road-numbers, and where and when he had spotted them. What he gathered was that steam engines had beautiful names, particularly those prepared for the black beauty contest organised by zonal railways. Not every steam engine was entitled to an individual name though. But what he discovered was that his zone had a name for each and every mainline steam engine. It was a perpetual mystery for him until his research on World War II China-Burma-India Theatre gave him a clue. His friend George had sent him a picture of his father serving the American Army's railway battalion in India posing with a wartime locomotive named Molly at Lumding. Perhaps that fashion of Americans naming their locomotives caught the eyes of the Assam Bengal Railway employees. So when the War was over, they retained that fashion till the steam locomotives lost their steam. They had a neighbour in their village who was a steam engine driver. He named his engine Aparajita, the unconquered. In his family life, he chose a lesser name for his daughter. Those breed of men did love their engines. They would lose the night's sleep over the trouble of their engine, but not when their child had caught a fever. An engine was not a metal pile for them, it was a kin. When it was the day, the day of the last run of the steam in 1997, the station master Mr. Das in their nearby station sobbed heavily as he waved his green for the last time to the engine he had been seeing all these years under his nose. How did he feel that day? Did he feel like M. Hamel in The Last Lesson? Or did he feel like the demise of the child he had been taking care of all those years?

Nairatmya returned to his hostel with a mixed bag of feelings and realisations. It was an unidentifiable mixture of de-ja-vu and ja-mais-vu. He could see how these diesel engines were going to repeat the same fate as the steam engines. He could foresee what was waiting for the diesel engines. His doctoral thesis had the least to do with these thoughts. That thesis would hardly capture any emotion from any sphere of railway life. All he intended to do through the research was to spend a couple of years understanding the railways and getting that doctoral degree as a byproduct. This does not embarrass him, neither does it disappoint. He knew from the beginning that his academic studies would not land him anywhere. However, the opportunity created during the process would be a long-term investment in some other form. People often misunderstand his hobby as a by-product of his research. But this is the other way around. Now, sitting in his room he was noting down the chain of thoughts before forgetting them. Just then Geoffrey Fernandes returned from somewhere and asked him for a cup of coffee. Evenings such as these are the times they share their cups of coffee and thoughts on things they feel like talking about.

Geoffrey is a lead guitarist in a band called 6th Mile Stone. Nairatmya knew the drummer of the band Vishnu even before he met Geoffrey. They share the same passion for railways. Perhaps this mutual friend forged a bond between Nairatmya and Geoffrey as well. Geoffrey asked him what he was writing about. On being told about the evening's events, Geoffrey remarked, "You should have met my grandpa. You would have loved talking to him."

– Is he a railway enthusiast?

– No. He used to work in the RDSO. In fact, my father is the first one in our family who is not into the railways.

Geoffrey's parents worked at IIT Roorkee. All Nairtmya knew was they hailed from Lucknow. But did not know that his grandfather was in RDSO.

– So I would love to. Where does he stay now? In Roorkee?

– No, he's six feet deep under now.

– Oh, I am sorry bro. I hadn't realise that.

– Our great-grandfather used to work in the railways in Quetta. That's in Pakistan now. After the Partition he decided to move into this side. So he was transferred to Palghat.

– Yes, I know. It's called Palakkad now. In Kerala.

– Yes. He married and retired from there and then my grandfather got the job in RDSO here in Lucknow.

– Does anyone live there in Kerala now?

– No the whole family moved here. But we do not have any home as such. Typical of Anglo-Indians. We are constant drifters. Anyway, moving was not a big thing for us Anglo-Indians. Because we didn't have any home. Someone had an English father whose home was not in India. Then living in railway colonies means you get staff quarters for a lifetime and no one bothers to get a home of their own. So finally we landed here in the RDSO colony. My father was born here. Again he and my mother moved to Roorkee. We have been living there since. Now after their retirement perhaps there will be a home.

– Just tell me one thing, are you people even Indian?

– Huh! What sort of question is that?

– No, I mean for citizenship documents, what kind of land ownership documents do you or can you produce? It's not funny man, we have this issue back there in my home state.

– Having Central Government employee documents has so far worked I guess.

– Yeah, probably. Perhaps it's a curse of the Anglo-Indians like the Jews to remain homeless. And it's also a benefit of being Anglo-Indian that no one questions citizenship.

– I don't know. Who knows tomorrow I might be questioned as doubtful Bangladeshi. But as of now, I am as safe as I have been.

– It's kind of funny that your great-grandfather was posted so far in the South from the extreme north of British India.

– That's the railway I presume.

– Yes, it is indeed. By the way, the other day I met another first-generation Anglo-Indian. He is the station master in Dilkusha. Mr. Michael Hill. He told me that he is the last of the first-generation Anglo-Indians in Northern Railways. His family history too, I now think, is somewhat similar to your family. He was born and brought up in Kharagpur. You know Kharagpur once had a huge Anglo-Indian, rather Anglo-European railway colony. But now he has settled down here in Lucknow.

– Take me someday to meet him.

– Yeah, definitely. He too likes football. He said he used to play for the district team. And he plays the saxophone. You two have a lot in common to talk about.

– Saxophone is kind of history now. Not too many people play that thing these days.

– Yeah. That's why I think you people are some preserved antiquities. Haha!

– Where is Raunak by the way? Haven't seen him this week.

– He's from another homeless family. So he has it in his blood to roam around. Right now he is on a tour to Rajasthan. Doing metre gauge sections before they disappear.

Raunak. Raunak Banerjee. Another quintessentially homeless soul. His family hails from Assam's Dhubri. His father moved into Lucknow for his job. They live in a rented house. Since his job is a government job, he is stuck here for the lifetime. And Nairatmya doesn't think they'll ever return to Assam. Once Nairatmya asked him where he felt at home to which he replied that Lucknow is their home now. They don't have a house of their own here, yet their home is here. They visit Dhubri every once in a while, but for Raunak that is just another trip. He never felt that home.

Raunak had expertise in understanding train routes. Every time any new train was introduced, Raunak would make a trip on the first run. Nothing on earth could dissuade him from those trips. When the Kolkata to Agra Express was introduced, he was the passenger on it. When the train arrived at Mughalsarai, it was forty minutes before time. Raunak therefore decided to get a haircut outside the station. And after the haircut, he boarded the same train and travelled to Agra. His trips were not mere trips. Those were adventures of their own sort. Sometimes he would drag Nairatmya to the station just to watch the crowds in trains. One summer evening they were sitting at the platform of Lucknow Junction. Mumbai-bound Pushpak Express was there in front of them. Raunak held the hand of Nairatmya and took him to a window of a general class coach. Nairatmya could see from outside that there was not an inch left inside the coach which was unoccupied. Every Mumbai-bound train has this scene. As Nairatmya reached the window, a gush of hot stinking air sent him dizzy. Raunak said, "That's the smell of general class, dada. This is just the evening. And all these people have tomorrow's daytime heat to face in the driest part of the country. Imagine their plight. I won't be surprised if a few of these people arrive dead in Mumbai." That was overcrowded indeed. But the next coach had no crowd. It was an air-conditioned coach. "This is our country dada, this is our country. We have both these sections of people, totally invisible to each other."

Nairatmya left Lucknow a decade ago. Raunak visited him twice since then. His last visit was when Nairatmya was to leave Guwahati to join the current position. Raunak just travelled all the way to click a photograph of Nairatmya at Guwahati railway station, ready to board the Jorhat Town bound Janshatabdi Express. No, Raunak didn't travel on that train that day and for that matter, he had never. He'd catch the Saraighat Express to Howrah a couple of hours after Nairatmya's departure. From there he was to catch one of the slowest trains in northern India – the infamous Bagh Express – to reach Lucknow. His travellings had been that much unusual. A direct train never pleased him. Even when Nairatmya was travelling to Phulera in Rajasthan to visit the salt panes of Sambhar Lake there, Raunak decided not to accompany him but meet him at Phulera through an unusual route. He went to Delhi by Lucknow Mail, then took Chetak Express to Churu, and then travelling by the metre gauge train to Jaipur and finally took another train from there to Phulera. That boy loved moving around instead of staying in one place. Every time Nairtamya decided to call him would mean a live reporting from the other side like which train he was currently travelling on or to where he was booking a ticket at that moment. Did he suffer from quintessential homelessness like a Marlovian hero or he was a nomadic in spirit? Nairatmya never got any answer to that.

Then gradually their phone calls became less frequent. Some five years ago they had a group trip to Payannur. Why did they choose to pay a visit to Payannur is another whimsical trip planning. Samar Hussain planned the trip. Raunak suggested that they should change trains and reach Payannur. Then returning to Mangalore they should head to Subrahmanya Road to travel by freight train to Sakleshpur. Samar Hussain was another train enthusiast of his own kind. For the love of trains, Samar had left his job in 2009. He was a living encyclopedia of railways. The whole trip was sponsored by the Railway Board. So they had the opportunity of travelling in engines and staying in Officer's Rest Houses. On that trip the locomotive rides were in hand experience which shattered all the romantic ideas of being a train driver. Nairatmya had travelled in the locomotive cab earlier too. He gained fair experience of driving it between Kanpur and Lucknow. But this trip from Subrahmanya Ghat to Sakleshpur was a terrible experience. The surrounding beauty of nature and hills with their romantic monsoon affairs failed to compensate for the discomfort. So that was perhaps how the railwaymen felt. They get to pass through the photographic landscapes, but their paramount working discomfort prevail upon everything. However, the stay at the Officers' Rest House at Sakleshpur opened with an unparalleled vista in the morning. From the hillock they saw the entire yard of the Sakleshpur station and the enchanting Hemavathi river flowing paralle to the yard. Now that was a picture to bring back home. That was the last trip they all did together. After that Samar's health started deteriorating, Raunak kept on travelling, and Nairatmya got sunk in his teaching.

Just then someone posted a picture of Southern Railway's Golden Rock Workshop planting a sapling where a plaque was installed which read 'In Loving Memory of Late Raunak Banerjee'. Raunak's homeless spirit found a permanent address in Golden Rock. It was the railways that made so many memories for them. Nairatmya just leaned back in his chair. He was about to post the photograph of the father-son duo on Facebook. Now he was wondering which photograph with Raunak would be a perfect tribute to that wandering soul. It won't be easy to find one. Raunak was camera shy, and yet some of the photographs he had of him are perhaps worth nothing but worth the memory of a lifetime – Raunak sitting at a window and scrutinising the working timetable to work out where their Mandovi Express would cross with the Gandhidham Express. Nairatmya never had any photograph of Raunak planning a trip sitting in his hostel room. But that is another picture he carries in his heart, like the picture of the father-son duo during the sunset hours.

CHAPTER TWO

Shadows on the Tracks

Keerthy Elza Tes Mathew

Murderer I am, condemned by fate's decree.
Stoic I've become.
Witnessing deaths,
A helpless victim of tragedies,
Haunting my weary soul
Murderer I am, though no blood stains my hands.
Proud I was,
Master of the iron serpent,
Guiding fearlessly,
Until one day...
Until one Day
I saw shadows wavering
In distance
Pixelated figures moving....
Spots of color it seemed
NO...it wasn't!!!
Despair impersonated it was....
Hands tremble, Heart quiver
Eyes shut; screams stifled,
Silent echoes in the air
Whispers linger....
Whistles whimper...

Apparitions haunt....
Shadows of despair....
Murderer I am,
condemned by fate's decree
Stoic I have become
Witnessing deaths,
Helpless victim of tragedies,
Haunting my weary soul
Murderer I am, though no blood stains my hands.
Clock ticks, Things change.
"Wisdom of the years..."
May this phrase justify my stoic heart.
Now, nothing hurts.
Habitual it has become
Time heals, Scars vanishes
Rephrasing....
Proud I am
Captain of the Iron horse
Savior I am
For multitudes, engulfed by fate's decree

CHAPTER THREE

Ticket Please

Swayama Sengupta

"So when I pull your pockets, you would buy me *badam*. Promise?"

"Oh, sure."

"Your *dadu* never kept his promise, though. When the hawker appeared selling peanuts, dalmoth, *and kochubhaja* in his shrill voice, which was quite distinctive of them, I gently tugged his pockets as 'agreed'. Once, twice, thrice…"

"But why not ask him directly?"

"Ask him in the presence of a bunch of strangers and let them know what a kid I was? Nope. But that was, probably, a better idea. As I pulled his Punjabi pocket for the fourth time, my father hurriedly folded his Statesman and declared, "Oh, yes, I remember buying the peanuts when you tug my pockets. See? I did not forget." Needless to say, I could feel curious looks and peeping heads while my six year old self, too proud to be a kid, focused at the rice fields outside wishing our stop to arrive. Even the hawker did not have to be summoned, he understood the assignment and handed me a pack of salted peanuts endearingly."

"That must have been a local train, right? I love express trains, the ones where you could enjoy an overnight journey…"

"…and consider the compartment as your home."

Raahi and her mother giggled.

"They do have their charms. Remember the time we were travelling to Kalimpong, and the family sharing our compartment?"

"Who could forget the unruly children swinging about the berths while the mother unpacked the luggage and handed out the father a Bermuda and a white tank top to be *at home*? Baba could not keep his cool when they strung a clothesline."

Karuna, Raahi's mother, wiped a tear away, "And why wouldn't he? They had even asked us to swap seats for the water dripped on their side. The ticket checker was taken aback when they demanded a refund on being warned, didn't he?

"He swore that he had never met a stranger family before," Amit remarked. "What are we discussing about today?"

"Trains and their quirks. Any funny anecdotes about them, *baba*?"

"Not sure about funny but I do recall once when I was travelling to Chakdaha with two bags stuffed with library books. I put one of them on the overhead bunker and found myself a seat. I got off the train without the other bag and realised it too late as I watched the train leaving the station, horrified. It was not wise enough to run as you could stumble and fall, so, I boarded another train headed in the same direction and reached Krishnanagar, the final halt."

"But isn't Krishnanagar dreaded for its crammed trains?"

"It certainly is, and that was yet another reason for my trouble. Luckily, I found the compartment and my bag, and was about to take it down when people screamed, children cried, a milk drum crashed, and I felt a few pair of strong hands grabbing my waist, "Do not touch that, *babu*. We are to vacate the compartment right now." And before I could say something, another voice added, "The RPF have been reported, they would be here any moment." I did not wish to move an inch without my bag but I found myself gradually being distanced from the bunker by the stream of people. I was late to college that day, had to present an explanation on behalf of my bag and pay for the spilt milk as well."

Raahi could barely stop laughing, "That's a pun fact right there. I do get the part about getting off trains. If you stand near the entrance, a stuffed compartment is sure to shove you out, the trick being you have to ask the one in front whether the passenger would be getting off on the same station."

"But trains are not always fun," Karuna commented grimly, "You might not remember it all as you were little, but it happened when we were on our way back from Varanasi. There were five of us and we were busy chatting about our time in Varanasi, the boat rides, the Ganga *aarti*, Chunar Fort, and deciding on the souvenirs to be gifted to neighbours. I do not remember the station but it was at around 7:30 that we noticed a man quietly seated on the side lower berth and stealing glances at us. I suppose, we were too happy to pay a heed to him and finished off dinner. Next morning, I was the first to wake up at 9, fresh and in high spirits to have a sound sleep when I reached out for my cell phone in my bag and found it wide open. The cell phone was not there, of course, which made me look at the side lower berth which was missing its passenger as well. I hurriedly woke you all up and made each check into the luggage. The damage was done; three cell phones, cash, and the souvenirs were all missing while the other belongings lay there, disheveled."

"Really? How did none of us have a clue? Did he...?"

"He most certainly did. Soon after finishing dinner, and I remember it still, I heard a rhythmic clap and repeated tap of palms. I thought it was *gutkha* then, but the fact that all of us dozed off immediately did mean we were being sprinkled something from afar as I sniffed a sweet scent. Good thing we reached home safe."

"The worst being we did not have any souvenirs to give to our neighbours," Amit pointed out. "Is that why the Chatterjees did not gift a souvenir to us when they came back from Darjeeling a month later?"

"Very funny", Karuna grimaced.

Amit slurped his tea, "Trains come with surprises, and they could meet you with your destiny."

"About that," Raahi straightened her spine, finally finding something to contribute, "on my way to the university, I encounter a beggar who sings Nazrul Geeti at the Kalyani Local every day. It was just the other day that I heard him sing a couple of songs on the request of a familiar looking lady. After a while, she handed him a card and told him to get in touch with her. I was later told that the lady was none other than Anjali Dasgupta, the renowned Nazrul Geeti singer. That left me wondering whether it was destiny and if it was, destinies are sweeter than movies."

"He rightfully deserved it," smiled Amit. "I think the best of my train journeys was when I travelled to college with my colleagues. As most of them have retired now, it is not fun anymore. Remember your Akhilesh *jethu*? He was hilarious with his witty remarks. Well, this might sound a little repulsive but we still have a good laugh about it. One day, while returning from college, we were discussing about how each of us had our own ways of finding students cheating. Only Akhilesh*da* did not participate, I followed his eyes and found him staring at a man picking his nose and a few minutes later heard him asking, "Anything invaluable in there, *dada*?"

"He really said that? The man must have been so embarrassed."

"He left his seat almost immediately and got off on the next station. There's more. Once, on our way back, Akhilesh*da* smiled pleasantly to a towering well built young man standing close to him:

- *Dada*, where are you going to get off?
- The station after the next.
- Would you like to have a seat? My colleague here would gladly give up his.
- I am fine, thank you.
- Are you sure? Your foot has been trampling mine for a while now so I would be a little relieved if you would please consider my humble offer.

"The thing is", Amit continued, "his tone maintained the language of a perfectly formal email while betraying a hint of anger. The man was huge. Akhilesh*da* did not have a choice. And no sooner did he disappear to the other side than Akhilesh*da* swore on him while desperately attempting to bring his "senseless foot back to senses".

Karuna put her tea aside and joined in, "Back in 1986, Doordarshan broadcasted a series called *Yatra*. It showed people from different regions, religions, professions, circumstances, boarding a train headed to Jammu from Kanyakumari. Throughout the journey, passengers assemble, defending themselves from dacoits, helping a woman deliver her baby, finding love, eventually becoming a huge family for a few nights. I guess Om Puri was right, "Life is like a train ride. You meet strangers on the train and become close to them. As you reach your destination and bid them adieu, you do feel sorry but the memories remain."

As the nostalgia loomed large in the room for a while, Raahi stretched a little, reached for her pencil case and took me out, "Good thing I have treasured this. You get paper tickets now. Why did they stop issuing these cardboard tickets? You could collect them; they were more durable, and looked vintage."

"Well, we can always talk about that later but for now, keep the ticket safe. It is not only a reminder of transition but a bygone era well cherished too. Besides, what are the stations printed on it?"

"Sealdah to Barrackpore."

"And the year?"

"1999. Wait, so, was this train the one which you, grandma and grandpa boarded to meet *ma* and her family in Barrackpore, *baba*?"

"Enough with the *adda*, back to studies", ordered Amit while hastily arranging the tea cups on the tray and darting a glance at Karuna who immediately looked away, humming,

Ei poth jodi na shesh hoye, tobe kyamon hoto tumi boloto...

(*What if this journey doesn't come to an end...?*)

As a grinning Raahi put me back in her pencil case, I felt my faded yellow texture and ashy prints cheer up. Is this what they think of me? I, a forsaken being, who have been reminiscing my favourite words, "Ticket please" in my prime, am regarded a vintage? I can only be grateful for my journey so far, and can barely wait to behold the next stop where bewildered techie kids would meet an older me beaming at them through my folds and crinkles.

CHAPTER FOUR

Echoes of the Iron Rails

Richa Biswal

The sun dipped below the horizon, casting long shadows over the sleepy town of Devapur. As twilight settled, the distant whistle of a train echoed through the quiet streets, a sound that had woven itself into the fabric of the town's history. The Devapur Express, with its polished iron body and elegant carriages, had once been the lifeline of the region, connecting the remote town to the bustling cities beyond.

At the heart of this story was Meera, a woman in her early sixties, who had spent her entire life in Devapur. The train station had always held a special place in her heart. It was where she had met her late husband, Rajiv, a railway engineer with a passion for the tracks that mirrored her own. Together, they had shared countless journeys, both literal and metaphorical, along the iron rails.

Meera stood at the edge of the platform, her eyes tracing the well-worn path of the tracks. The station, though no longer bustling with the energy of its heyday, still exuded a quiet charm. The waiting room, with its wooden benches and old clock, was a relic of a bygone era. As she watched the approaching train, memories flooded her mind, each one more vivid than the last.

The Devapur Express pulled into the station with a gentle hiss, its brass fittings gleaming in the fading light. The conductor, a young man named Anil, greeted Meera with a warm smile. "Evening, Mrs. Sharma. Taking another trip down memory lane?"

Meera nodded, her eyes twinkling with a mixture of nostalgia and anticipation. "You know me too well, Anil. There's something magical about these tracks. They hold so many stories."

As she boarded the train, Meera found her favorite seat by the window. The compartment was cozy, with plush seats and dim lighting that created an intimate atmosphere. She settled in, the rhythmic clatter of the wheels beneath her feet a familiar and comforting sound.

The train began to move, gliding smoothly out of the station and into the night. Meera gazed out the window, watching the landscape change from the quaint streets of Devapur to the open fields and rolling hills beyond. Each passing scene triggered a memory, taking her back to moments she had cherished.

In her mind's eye, she saw the day she and Rajiv had first met. It was a crisp autumn morning, and she had been on her way to visit her grandmother in the neighboring town. Rajiv had been there, working on the tracks, his face smeared with grease and a broad smile on his lips. They had struck up a conversation, and before she knew it, they were inseparable.

Their love had blossomed on the rails, with every journey deepening their bond. They had traveled to distant cities, explored quaint villages, and shared countless sunsets from the windows of the Devapur Express. Even after Rajiv had passed away, the train remained a connection to their shared past, a vessel of memories that Meera treasured dearly.

As the train sped through the countryside, Meera's thoughts turned to the people she had met on her journeys. There was Ananya, a young artist from Kolkata, who had shared her sketches and dreams of opening an art gallery. And Vikram, an engineer from Bengaluru, whose stories of building bridges and railways had fascinated her. Each encounter had enriched her life, adding new dimensions to her understanding of the world.

The train slowed as it approached a small station, and Meera's thoughts returned to the present. She noticed a young couple boarding the train, their faces alight with excitement. They reminded her of herself and Rajiv, full of hope and anticipation for the adventures that lay ahead. She watched them find their seats, their laughter and whispered conversations filling the compartment with a sense of warmth and possibility.

The journey continued, weaving through the night as the train carried its passengers toward their destinations. Meera's mind wandered to the stories she had read about the railway's historical significance. The Devapur Express was not just a means of transportation; it was a symbol of connection and progress. It had played a crucial role in the development of the region, bringing people together and facilitating the exchange of goods and ideas.

She thought of the times when the train had been a lifeline during periods of hardship. During the war, it had transported soldiers and supplies, bridging the gap between the home front and the battlefields. In times of economic struggle, it had carried workers to factories and farms, sustaining communities and fostering resilience. The train had witnessed the highs and lows of human experience, bearing silent witness to the unfolding history.

As the train rolled on, Meera's reverie was interrupted by a sudden jolt. The lights flickered, and the train came to an unexpected stop. The passengers exchanged puzzled glances, and Anil appeared in the doorway, his expression calm but serious.

"Ladies and gentlemen, it seems we have a minor technical issue. We'll be stopped here for a short while as we resolve it. Please remain seated, and we'll keep you updated."

Meera felt a pang of anxiety but quickly reminded herself of the countless times she had faced similar situations with Rajiv by her side. She decided to make the best of the moment, striking up a conversation with the young couple seated across from her.

"Hello, I'm Meera. Looks like we're in for a bit of an adventure," she said with a smile.

The couple introduced themselves as Priya and Karan, newlyweds on their way to a honeymoon destination. They were eager to hear about Meera's experiences and listened intently as she shared stories of her travels with Rajiv.

As they talked, Meera noticed the camaraderie that had formed among the passengers. Strangers were exchanging stories, offering snacks, and reassuring each other. The temporary halt had transformed the compartment into a microcosm of shared humanity, where connections were forged, and kindness prevailed.

After what felt like an eternity, the train's lights stabilized, and the engine roared back to life. Anil reappeared, his smile returning. "We're all set, folks. Thank you for your patience. We'll be on our way shortly."

As the train resumed its journey, Meera felt a renewed sense of gratitude for the iron rails that had carried her through so many chapters of her life. The temporary interruption had served as a reminder of the resilience and strength inherent in every journey, whether smooth or fraught with challenges.

The landscape outside the window began to change once again, signaling their approach to Meera's destination. She gathered her belongings, feeling a bittersweet mix of emotions. As much as she cherished her memories, she knew it was essential to continue making new ones, to keep moving forward.

The train pulled into the station, and Meera stepped onto the platform, inhaling the crisp night air. She waved goodbye to Priya and Karan, wishing them a lifetime of adventures and happiness. As she walked away, she felt the comforting presence of Rajiv beside her, his spirit alive in every whistle of the train and every whisper of the iron rails.

The Devapur Express departed, leaving behind a station that held countless stories of love, loss, and transformation. Meera knew that the journey was far from over. As long as the tracks stretched into the horizon, there would always be new paths to explore, new connections to forge, and new tales to tell. And so, with a heart full of memories and a spirit open to the future, she continued her journey, ever guided by the echoes of the iron rails.

CHAPTER FIVE

The Drunk Train

Arnab Chatterjee

That day we take the train drunk with life
   To return Home after a long hustle:
   All the faces silently sing their strife
   While leaning on each like a ruffle.
   Some keep staring out of the windows
   Waiting for the familiar trees and lights,
   While some keep dealing cards to travel time.
   The wooden panes have turned into pillows
   Where the little boy has reached the heights
   In the silence of the rainless clime.
   They are drunk from life as their eyes speak
   In a language similar to ours -
   Yesterday took seconds to cross the creek
   Today we are travelling for hours!
   They are now mourning with droopy yawn,
   And dreaming to lay down and let go
   Of this costume heavy with broken stars.
   They die every day; in the next reborn,
   Just like the insignificant Pluto,
   Life is a great tapestry of scars.
   By the doors, waits an old woman, sitting
   With her unsold fruits to fill her night -

In the corner, the lonely boy waiting
For one blue tick from his life's light.
Another one brew envy in mind
As the rival snatches focus from
The two pretty souls and revives the dead.
He stays silent with sorrows of a kind
World destined to die in beats of drum,
Echoing the continuous dread.
Some lost their all, some gained too many
Within a click of trade among the flea;
Then there are some with music of any
Making rhymes and stories from what they see -
A mother hums with the clanking handle
While the child drifts off in the tender arms
Conjuring their safe and secure home;
Too drunk to see the Begger with Sandel
In the hands - crawling to save from the harms
Pushed upon him and his freedom to roam.
The lewd posters that tell future, flap
On the corners, barely hanging by;
Like the weeny fleas fallen for the trap
Set by the lights with a flickering lie.
And in the next day, they will be replaced
By another group boarding this train
After the day's toil, finding the rest.
They too once dreamed in a train unfazed
And sober; but now, they have a stain
Of unseen burdens hanging by the chest.
Some leaves relieved with each passing station,
Some boards to let their tale end for the day,
The rest keep waiting for their location
With their drunk bodies, letting it sway.
Still one hawker sells the last batch of nuts,
When one other drinks water from his stacks,
Then another sings in the microphone

To earn the last penny to fill the guts.
They know they will have to take these tracks
Again, to get drunk again, and groan.
We fail to see the moon and the stars
Embracing us as the night passes,
As we remain trapped behind the bars
Of the windows, blurry with scratched glasses.
Though fraught with feelings, the journey takes us
Closer - to the station bidding each
With a shared promise of morning dew.
With a final shake, some leaves without fuss,
Rest will follow one by one as they reach
Their time and bid with a humbling adieu.

CHAPTER SIX

The Lost Destiny

Smeha John Machado

"Careful, the steps are slippery," said the little girl to her grandfather, who was an octogenarian like me. For an instance I thought those precious words were for me but it greeted the latter who had followed me from behind. I got into my compartment, reached for my seat and placed my luggage. Hoping for this monotonous journey to end quickly, I turned to see that little girl hopping joyfully beside her grandpa, holding his hand securely. This brought back the blessed years with my own grandchildren who were later restricted from visiting me. She carefully guided that old man into his seat and suddenly he was encompassed by an army of his own! The entire aura of that dull compartment echoed with their elated voices and light-hearted jokes. I was convinced at this point that this man is dearly loved by his family. I gently tapped my suffering envious heart to calm down, persuading that poor thing with promises that I am financially stable with a secured social status, having lived life to the fullest and waiting for a joyful end. It tapped back, my heart did, it reminded me of a void in it which had never been filled for the past sixty years. The tapping continued forcing me into the present, I looked up to see those hands which tapped me, I was asked to show my ticket.

This 'joyful family' whom I've nicknamed by now, was asked to hush their tones since bedtime was nearing. The train slowly increased its pace, the children and their parents immediately switched off the lights lowered their frolic noises and the entire clan retreated to whispers and soft giggles. Since they were restricted from loud entertainments the little ones gathered around that old man. With their eyes gleaming from the only light at the end of the compartment, the children whispered, "Can we Grandpa?". He replied, "Not sure kids, it's time to hit the hay." I understood their statements immediately. They wanted their old man to tell stories which led to dreams filled with enchanting forests, dangerous pirates, raging monsters and valiant heroes dreamt by those little souls. The old man yielded to those little squeals and began his narration. I eagerly switched my pillow to the other side of my seat, kind of eavesdropping but never mind, who would not want a story to cover up this monotonous track tale of mine. He began as he should, "Once upon a time..." the little girl interrupted, "we don't need that Grandpoppzz, we've heard a lot of that, why don't you begin with some lively introspective thoughts of a hero maybe in a difficult situation?" Meanwhile I slithered to the edge of my seat, my body rattling to the rhythm of the train, I laughed at the little one's smartness she doesn't want a damsel in distress, she wants the roles to be reversed. "Alright then, wish granted princess," he began whispering the dialogues of the characters with proper intonations along with his third person narration. And so started the story:

'I should have... No I shouldn't have...well, it is a good decision to get everyone's share...no, I shouldn't have taken this rash decision,' said Ravi while his great bead of sweat fell on the matchbox consisting only two matchsticks. Earlier that morning a pack of young men had decided to spend the night at a ruined Tavern, which almost looked like a posh guesthouse of someone who must have had a reputation before the king. It was located in the woods near the village named Angara. These young fellows had come to Angara to load goods and get a day's pay. Sadly, they got their pay but not trusted enough to get a place to stay. So, Mahesh came up with the idea of staying at this ruined inn. The more the villagers warned them the more they got excited to see what was in it.

'Perfect', exclaimed Ravi who had lit the candle in his first attempt and grinned for having saved the only hope, that is, the other matchstick. He took a look around the little yet well-furnished room but now, all the owner's aesthetics have become desperate preys for the moths, bats and cobwebs. Even in its rusted look, Ravi could feel the room having its own soul and each spooky ends had tales to tell it's new visitor. Ravi shivered partly due to cold and partly due to fear. He cursed his friends who had suggested for the bet and cursed his very soul for agreeing to get everyone's pay in the morning if he had the nerve to stay ALONE in that ruin. "No idiot would agree for it", gasped the little children but that old man grinned and continued with his tale. Since Mahesh knew Ravi had a necessity, he was clever enough to make an idiot out of Ravi.

Ravi tried to calm down but his mind wouldn't, it rehearsed all the spooky tales, the villagers told them about the inn. He suffered to think about the master's wailing lady love and the master himself, how would he react to a visitor relaxing on his couch? Ravi gasped and immediately pounced out of the sagging couch. But deep down he knew his friends wouldn't leave him for the money bag and he was the one to agree to the bet, no one compelled him.

'Oh, come on! don't you know, he's a sturdy fellow and will accomplish whatever he gets in his mind, he has his own stupid sentiments and his poor family is desperately in need of money So we need to vacate soon", Mahesh warned the others. "And if he comes out in the morning, sane without getting traumatized ...then being victorious in the bet we forced him into his demand will be for all our money', cried one of the friends.

"How cruel of them, Grandpa", said the children. "Yes indeed", said he and retreated to his story.

Ravi counted the bats on the ceiling and was ready to confront any hanging mistresses or a burnt beauty or even a werewolf. Oh! Forget about the last one, human brains could play tricks. The wax melted soon and a low-lit flame was clinging on it for its dear life. Ravi wanted to sleep before it would go out or perhaps before someone would put it out, he shrieked at this thought. The winds blew heavily carrying a melancholic tune filling the air, the room went dark.

A similar gentle breeze gushed through our windows while the train crossed through the fields. I could hardly listen now since the train rattled my brain and so did my neighbour's snores. I tried and then heard him speak

As the wind blew away the only light in his room, Ravi crouched at one corner, shivering, to his surprise, he witnessed a lit candle near the ceiling and he could see the bats shimmering in the dark room. He searched for his pockets, the matchstick which he had saved earlier was missing! 'Dear me', exclaimed Ravi , he fainted. Morning rays hit his face, drenched in his clothes, Ravi woke up and found the room serene with a fresh scent of paddy fields filling it. He jumped victoriously and left the room without turning back ...the cruelty it showed him last night! To the villagers' astonishment, this young lad came out alive from the ill-omened tavern. But Ravi's triumph turned to remorse when he heard a passerby discuss about a group of young men been waylaid and killed and how they always knew this tavern and the forest was an accursed one. Ravi's heart pounded and he felt a great vacuum, not because of his uncelebrated victory over the bet, but because he realized the monsters WITHOUT are much crueller than the imagined monsters WITHIN. Because those thieves took the life of his dear friends.

"That was wonderful Grandpa", exclaimed the children and gave him bedtime kisses one by one. "Not even a single friend who betrayed Ravi survived that robbery, you know, you reap what you sow", said one child. "Kid, that judgement is NOT commendable" smirked the old man. "Sorry grandpa, Good night."

"Ravi... sorry I didn't mean to... I was just a kid back then...but you believed me" ...I woke up mumbling, to the smell of savoury breakfasts being circulated amidst my co passengers. I was asked too but I refused to buy. The man insisted that their train canteen foods were worthwhile and healthy for an ancient like me. I was not an old man anymore. I never felt the same since the previous night's story because I didn't hear that old man's ending. I never knew how I slept through the night. I desperately wanted to know the ending because my memory had somehow brushed up something and played tricks with me.

The train arrived at my station. I walked past the old man. Suddenly he called me by my name "Mr. Maheshkumar, is this your wallet." I grabbed it with haste and uttered a thank you under my breath and climbed down in haste. Why did I feel guilty I didn't know the answer to it. I got down on my own with no beloved family to pick me up. I sat down on one of the benches.

As the train left slowly, I looked at him and he grinned at me as if he knew me. I knew something was off when my brain had remembered a different ending to his story. My Goodness, it was Ravindran...my dear friend Ravindran whom I betrayed that night outside the tavern for money! His smile pierced through, like a spear, right down my throat. I reassembled my distorted memory. As each compartment flashed by me, I started growing much younger. Next train arrived at the station, amidst a crowded platform sat a young boy with the bag full of hard-earned money hoping to escape by catching the train. I left him, made him believe we were all killed. The pain he would have felt of losing his friends, and the pain of betrayal after he would have heard about our existence. Poor Ravi, oh no, poor me. I'm lost now, but he is found!

CHAPTER SEVEN

Tobacco Tale

Sakshi Nain Bishnoi

Do you even know how much I missed you on the train back home? How much I missed your presence, your laughter, your ingenuous baby voice, your tears. How does one come to reconcile this distance every three months? Is there a protocol that I am not aware of? Can I just switch off my brain and put the thought of you into a light corner, where I can just sleep thinking about you, but not miss you terribly? I reached a couple of days back, it's almost as if I have been working like a zombie, sleeping as if a movie is going in my head, completely anxious not getting any rest at all. Cleaning the dishes, mopping the floor. Cooking, reading. Cleaning the dishes, mopping the floor. Debating between opening the door to let some air in, or not, to stop warm, suffocating wind from entering my lungs and altering my inherent physiology. Cleaning the dishes, mopping the floor.

Indian Railways are formidable. There is the possibility of finding the love of your life, and paan stains on your seat. Do you remember? You came with me to the train station. While waiting for the train, you bought me chips and cake and yogurt. We were happy and anxious, present and absent, trying to savor the last moments of us, physically together, with this looming exorbitant implication that I was about to leave soon. The train, leisurely standing on the platform had the evidential claim on the tangibility of our love.

Couldn't you have just boarded the train with me? Why did I have to leave you standing there, waving goodbye? In that moment, who was more stranded, you or I?

On the upper berth of a sleeper coach in mid-June, I lay awake, struggling against the oppressive heat that made sleep impossible. The noise compounded my discomfort—a man on the opposite berth, stripped down to his vest and shorts, was absorbed in scrolling through propaganda reels in the aftermath of the election. Desperation clawed at me. I had to look for something, something to keep me focussed, something to keep me from peeling my skin off with my bare hands, blood running out, just to feel a semblance of some liquidy coolness to help me sleep.

Then I saw it—the cinematic effect that it embodied threatened my sense of reality for a second.. Two young men, likely in their early twenties judging by the smoothness of their hands, shared an RAC seat. They could have been forty with exceptional skincare routines, but the rolled-up sleeves and dark maroon georgette shirt in the height of summer screamed twenties to me and I'd rather stick to that.

From my angle, I could only see their hands up to their elbows. One was engrossed in his phone while the other procured a tobacco sachet from a train vendor and began preparing it in his hand. His hands looked tender. As if the only labor that they were accustomed to was this. And the labor of stolen intimacy.

He gently placed the prepared tobacco into the other's palm. The second man received it with reverence, his hand stretched out as if accepting a divine offering. Their hands held each other for twenty seconds, racing through a web of intermittent desires, promises and heartbreak. The hands broke the web. They went to their separate places. Now. I can just see their legs dangling off the train seat, far apart, sweaty, wanting for more, trying for less.

In the famous French films, or even your mainstream Indian movies, cigarette butted its way into the romantic discourse. The lovers would smoke, so would the philosophers. I never thought tobacco would be the cinematic surrogate. But here I am, thinking about the tale of tobacco transfer, as a romantic, albeit slightly melancholic, moment of my dreams.

This borrowed sense of adventure. This borrowed sense of intimacy. Stolen, but intimacy nonetheless. Do I need to question my moral standpoint, being a voyeur, living off of a moment reserved for those two people? If I would've talked to them, would they have given me permission to think about them, to write about them? To make them a part of my own clandestine meditation about love, intimacy and separation. Do I want to burst this, my romantic bubble for some enlightened epistemic elegy? I did have the whole train ride to think about it, but I don't think I have reached any conclusion whatsoever.

CHAPTER EIGHT

Station One to Infinity

Nikitha Nelson

Huffing like a grandfather,
It moved slowly and detached
Reminding me of a dandy local
Smoking with a duty-free pipe.

The rickety tracks posed a challenge
For this vintage mass to gain momentum.
Gazing outside only to meet
The longing eyes of the bystanders;
They search frantically for those
Whom they hold a care for.

Station One carries my past
The journey will secure me a future
The destination? I'm not sure.

I only remember flashes
I did catch sight of a few things:
The fields waiting lustfully for hands to reap
Pretty homes left for decay
Dogs sleeping like carpets before doors
A cold sea sedated in oil and moss.

The seagulls are cautious to screech
I am reminiscent of what became of me
And this journey extends deeper
Into infinite tracks.

CHAPTER NINE

Chugging Toward Fate: Love and Farewell

Itrat Khan

Madam, I can take your luggage and get you to the train within 8 minutes. I know a shortcut; you can avoid the checking process, too. Without a second thought and asking about his charges, I asked him to carry my luggage to the train. HA1coach, D cabin, I asserted again. Exhausted from running, we finally reached our cabin. As soon as I settled my things under the seats, I looked up for my seat. Excuse me, can you please shift? That's mine, lower berth. I looked at him, but he didn't. A young man busy eating his parathas dipped in chutney, unbothered of giving heed to a beautiful woman standing in front of him. We rarely see such creatures, too fond of food to look around for opportunities. With his mouth full of morsel, he replied, hmm..hmm. I patiently waited. He went to wash his hands and then came back. This is how a stranger sharing the cabin with us can tell a story to others, but from my perspective, it was a completely different one.

This man, sitting there and enjoying his parathas, had always been a lover of food. I knew him not just from this train journey but from our school days. If it were just us, I might have embraced him for our twelve-hour journey. But here, in this train cabin, our shared history seemed to fade into the background, replaced by the hustle and bustle of the journey. Still, that one glimpse of him took me 13 years back. From when he knew what could light my face up, he definitely left no hook unturned to make me feel special. I wanted to stop him, ask him to sit beside me so I could share his shoulder and cry for the past years, to feel the warmth of his heart but kept my wishes in my heart: unspoken and unheard. He sat beside me, having just returned from the lavatory. I felt a mix of shyness and hesitation, unable to meet his gaze. Phone calls absorbed his attention, likely updating his whereabouts to someone—perhaps his fiancée. When he finally looked my way, I mustered the courage to request water. To my surprise, he handed me his bottle, and we exchanged a small smile. It was a fleeting moment, yet it left an indelible mark—a silent connection amidst the chaos of travel. His smile held secrets—of missed chances, of untold stories. And in that shared moment, I glimpsed the possibility of something more. I couldn't figure out his feelings and thoughts but I wish if I had known, it could have been better for me to express my feelings. He asked how are you? I smiled and replied great! I couldn't digest his constant messages to his fiancee. You see, his attention has been shifted to some other woman. How could men move on so fast? I questioned myself. Fiancee, I asked. Yes, he replied. MHMM great! Leave that. he held my hand and said 13 yrs, tera saal baad mil rahe hum. I replied, "Oh, it's been so long, isn't it? Trying to be as formal as possible. I think it was not me but my jealousy that was making me sound rude. That touch took me back to our first-morning walk, where I held his hand. He was too timid to do that, so I took the initiative. Guess what? After that, he didn't wash his hands for the day. Just to have that essence of my skin in his. 2012 dawned with the promise of something extraordinary—a morning etched in soft hues, where the sun peeked through the mist, casting a golden glow upon our lives. It was a day that would forever alter the course of our intertwined destinies.

Three days before our memorable walk, amidst laughter and twinkling fairy lights, he knelt before me—a declaration of love wrapped in vulnerability. His eyes, wide and earnest, held a universe of emotions. The room faded into insignificance as he fumbled for words, the weight of his heart evident in every syllable. "I Love you" His voice trembled, and I wondered if the universe held its breath. The question hung in the air, a fragile thread connecting past, present, and future. And in that suspended moment, I glimpsed eternity—the merging of two souls, each carrying their own scars and dreams.

"Say it," I urged, my heart pounding. "Say it loudly and clearly."

And he did. His raw and unfiltered voice echoed through the room, a proclamation transcending time and space. "I love you," he declared, the syllables etching into my soul. It was more than a promise; it was a covenant—a binding of hearts, a leap into the unknown.

The obstacles—the ones that seemed insurmountable in our teenage years—now blurred into insignificance. I said yes—not just to a proposal, but to a lifetime of shared sunrises and whispered secrets. Our love story, like that beautiful morning in 2012, defied logic. It was messy, imperfect, and utterly ours.

Let's eat makhana, he said. My bubble got blasted. I took some of it and thanked him. I had always loved the essence of chai, chand, and manpasandida shakhs? I extended a simple invitation: "Would you like some tea?" His eyes met mine—a silent acknowledgement—and he nodded.

As the train carved its way through the landscape, trees blurred into a verdant tapestry. Moonlight filtered through the window. It was as if the universe conspired to bless our fleeting connection—a celestial spotlight illuminating our shared moment. I reached for his hand, fingers intertwining. I felt the promise of something like a bridge across time and space. His shoulder became my sanctuary; I rested my head against it, inhaling the scent of longing. The ache of unfulfilled desires melted away, replaced by the warmth of his presence. While I could sense his heartbeat, I questioned myself again.

Did he feel it too—the love, the charm that defied reason?

We didn't need grand declarations or elaborate gestures. The train carried us forward, and we surrendered to its rhythm. Words hung unspoken, yet our hearts conversed—a language older than time. In that shared silence, I found solace—a refuge from a world that demanded explanations. He looked at me and asked kitna time hai abhi? ye train late kyu nhi horahi hai. I smiled. My heart was assured that it was not just me but that he too was enjoying the moment. He asked me to stand up. I did. We hugged each other. Yes, we did. Sat again to continue something with the silence. A silence that was more like a regret of not being together. So, do you think we could have made it? I mean, if we hadn't broken up at that time. He questioned.

His question hung like a fragile thread, tugging at memories long buried. "Could we have made it?" he asked, his eyes tracing the contours of my face. Maybe yes, maybe no—the answer, like the tracks stretching into infinity, eluded us. Our love story was woven from disparate threads—his laughter, my tears, my reality his fantasy, his unconditional love and mine unwavering support. We were rebels, defying the boundaries of religion and tradition. Our love was a clandestine affair—a secret whispered to the stars, etched into the folds of time.

"If he had taken a stand," I mused, my gaze drifting toward the departing train. Perhaps that was the crux—the moment when love demanded courage. But he wavered, caught between loyalty and longing. Like a fragile bird, his love fluttered against the cage of convention. And so, we unravelled—a tapestry of what-ifs and almost. The station clock ticked relentlessly, measuring our heartbeats. "Not letting me go at any cost," I whispered, my breath mingling with the scent of jasmine. But love, it seemed, had its price—a toll we paid in tears and silence.

"It's okay," I assured him, my fingers brushing against his. "Now it's over." The words tasted bitter, like unripe fruit. Yet, they held a strange sweetness—the acceptance of impermanence. Like the seasons, our love had its time—a fleeting bloom before the inevitable fall. Our religion was different, and our paths were divergent. He prayed in temples while I sought divinity in sunsets and whispered confessions. Our love was a heresy—an altar built on stolen moments and clandestine glances. We were star-crossed, our constellations misaligned. With us moving closer to our destination, our shared past—the stolen kisses, the moonlit promises—became a relic. But it was a good past, one we respected—a chapter etched in the annals of our souls.

I realized love was not about permanence; it was about the courage to leap, even when the chasm yawned wide.

"Chai, chai, chai..." The tea seller's sing-song call pierced the quiet. He shuffled down the aisle, balancing a tray of steaming cups. His face bore the etchings of countless mornings—the lines of resilience and quiet acceptance.

He checked his phone. "1.30 hours more," he remarked, his voice a low murmur. I nodded. And then, as if orchestrated by fate, my phone rang. My three-year-old stirred, his tousled hair a mirror of his father's. He looked handsome, intelligent, and undeniably cute. He resembled his father—the same crinkling eyes, the way he tilted his head when lost in thought. Without shame, I marvelled at this genetic echo—a bridge between past and present.

I answered the call. "Thought of reminding you about me," my dear husband said. His voice—a balm to my restless soul—held the weight of years. I smiled, graceful in my acceptance. "I love you," I replied.

His call was a bell—a summons from the present, pulling me from the sepia-toned reverie. The past, a utopia now, existed nowhere but within us. "It's okay," I whispered, my fingers tracing the frost-kissed window. "We just need to trust God's plan." The past is a utopia. Perhaps utopias exist not in the past, but in the grace with which we embrace what lies ahead.

I again questioned myself, what if I couldn't have adjusted to the new culture? What if my parents were heartbroken, never to recollect their broken pieces. Everything happens for good. Ah, I looked up at him with the same warmth, but this time, I was content with my life and everything without any question about the past. By this time we reached, I took my luggage out. He joined. He kissed my kid, and for the last time, he held my hand, only to disappoint me by not signing the song

--Abhi na jao chodkar ye dil abhi bhara nhi.. (That was one of my fantacy).

Like the train tracks, our love story stretched into infinity—a journey of longing and release. And so, I carry that memory—an unspoken bond woven into the fabric of my life for forever.

CHAPTER TEN

The Muted Wagon

Devika Vinod

Unclasped, hanging to the bones,
Flesh of memories, whole of life.
Yearning for a stop, finite period,
She went on her life, bearing lives.
The rails were set for her, in ironclad,
Not the heiress, but knew the course.
Endless paths could never surface
In the face of her rootless sojourn.
Shards of her soul detrained covertly,
Leaving behind all that she claimed.
Left abode, those pieces, not in harmony,
The tracks let them begone
While she feared to hold them close.
Tracks never taken, dreams undreamt,
Rules obeyed, all lost, all dust,
Along the muted journey.
People, that's what she hauled with her,
Carriage of their wishes, ailments and fret,
Relayed along with her skeletal wagon.
Wheels rattled, all the way along.
Tunnel brimmed with darkness,
Another phase of life, she thought,

A blind path for her blind journey.
With echoes of whistle it moved, the wagon.
Onward it went, beyond reasons for others
Without words to make sense, eyes shut,
Winding rails could never belong in
Any direction that she moved on.
Finally the last station, yearning to halt
She tried, to finally end the void self.
Name, as she was called, smeared,
Unrecognisable to the core, the skeleton.
Laden with regret, the chasm,
What she calls as her soul, infested
With the plague of undying dreams,
There lies the wagon, unable to move
For the first time in her lifetime.
Last breath of smoke added to the fog,
The weather wiped that away, in silence
There lies the muted wagon, soullessly.

CHAPTER ELEVEN

Whispers of the Iron Rails

Richa Biswal

Beneath the sky's resplendent dome,
Where horizons whisper and dreams roam,
The iron serpent winds its way,
Through valleys deep and hills of clay.
A chariot of steel and grace,
It carves a path, a timeless trace,
Bearing souls on quests profound,
Through echoing pasts and future sound.
The engines hum a mystic tune,
Underneath the silver moon,
Where travelers, in night's embrace,
Find solace in the fleeting space.
In carriages of old and new,
Where whispers mingle, soft and true,
Tales of yore and dreams unfurled,
In this moving, breathing world.
A tapestry of lives entwined,
On tracks of fate, in journeys lined,
With every clatter, every sway,
A story blooms, a life's ballet.
The romance of the railway calls,
Through verdant fields and ancient halls,

Of castles grand and city lights,
Of tranquil days and restless nights.
To lovers lost in twilight's glow,
With hearts alight, and spirits aglow,
The train's embrace, a gentle sigh,
Their hands entwined, as stars pass by.
Yet, not all tales are hearts entwined,
For in the shadows, secrets bind,
Mysteries hidden in the night,
Where shadows dance in fleeting light.
Adventures spark in every bend,
Where courage, fate, and fortunes blend,
From rugged peaks to oceans wide,
The train a stage, where fates collide.
Trains, the binders of the land,
Threads of iron, strong and grand,
They knit the far, the near, the known,
In one great, endless, heaving moan.
But with each mile of track they lay,
They bear the weight of social clay,
Of politics and human strife,
Of movements that reshape our life.
They've seen the tears of parting souls,
As loved ones leave for distant goals,
They've heard the cries of freedom's song,
And roared with strength, against the wrong.
In every station, every stop,
In bustling towns, on mountain tops,
A microcosm, life unfolds,
With tales as rich as gold untold.
So ride the rails, and seek your truth,
Embrace the old, discover youth,
For in the journey, hearts align,
In rhythms of the rail's design.
And as the iron serpent flows,

Through seasons' change, through sun and snow,
Remember this, oh wandering soul,
The train connects, and makes us whole.
Through personal quests and dreams on wing,
Through history's chords and songs we sing,
The train, a vessel of our time,
Whispers tales in every chime.
So let us ride these rails divine,
Where paths of past and future twine,
And in their gentle, rhythmic roll,
Find the whispers of our soul.

CHAPTER TWELVE

Journey of Reflection: Tracks of Change

Rahul Bajpai

His childhood in town was simply like a big book, where every day turned into an adventure in itself. Rahul would spend hours exploring the woods, climbing trees, and chasing after butterflies with his laughter ringing through the air. Young as he was, he had always been curious about life beyond his hometown's boundaries; he could spend long hours with maps and books on other countries far away. As years passed by, his ambitions changed. He performed well in school because of his determination and hard work that set him apart from other students in his class. But despite of all his academic achievements, he still knew he wanted to live in the fast-paced life of the city with its unlimited opportunities for living. At some point, it came time for him to say goodbye to his hometown so as to chase his dreams; at this time, there were mixed feelings of joy and fear within himself since he had spent all days and nights together with people who know him well around these streets. The familiarity of home provided him comfort while enticement of city-life was irresistible to disregard. With sorrow etched deeply in his soul but a heart full of hope, town that had made him became history as he opened another page in life.

As he sat by the window of a fast moving train, his reflection combined with the landscape which was moving and sliding past as the train passed through the village. The rhythmic clatter of wheels against tracks filled the air, a soothing melody that accompanied his thoughts. As he looked on, green fields faded into lines up trees, whose foliage rustled in the wind like murmurs from history. To Rahul, this compartment represented life itself with its varied passengers. Opposite him sat an old man absorbed in reading a book; his aged hands turning pages with skilled dexterity. What stories lay behind those pages? Love stories? Stories of pain? Stories of hope? While the train rode on, Rahul's mind wandered to his personal narrative. It was an important day in his youth as he was headed to another city for a job interview. Though leaving familiar streets in his hometown wasn't all bad news; yet he couldn't wait to embrace possibilities ahead. A few stations later a young lady entered carrying guitar case; her presence injected new energy into the coach.. Her name was Maya, and she had a quiet confidence, a thing he found intriguing. They began talking and soon enough he became engrossed in her stories about her musical escapades and artistic inclinations. The sun had gone down by now, causing the landscape to be bathed in warm light. The heavens were changing into a palette of lively hues which painted the earth with golds and reds. A sense of peace flowed over him as if telling him that whatever that lay ahead would turn out fine.

The train eventually came to a stop at the station. Rahul thanked it all within his heart for this literal journey or otherwise. He stepped outside onto the platform; took in deep breaths with sharp evening air filling his lungs up with coolness. It is time to start another phase after learning lessons from the train ride and its passengers who have come across his way.

CHAPTER THIRTEEN

Unfolding the Symphony of the Track

Ligia Nazareth

Travelling by train transcends both space and time. One of the most appealing aspects of train travel is its ability to create a new perspective of the world around us. It evokes a sense of wonder and nostalgia to 90's kids just like me. The rhythmic chug of a train engine serves as a symphony of possibility, inviting us to explore the world with open hearts and curious minds. Embarking on a two-day business trip to Delhi via the Nizamuddin Express promised an immersive experience filled with cultural richness, ideological crises and romantic chimes.

As the train departs from Quilon station, my heart slipped a beat. It was my first time in AC compartment and could never feel my feet. Well, the premium services provided in the train was mind-blowing and I even felt like I should have taken my cousins also with me... My mind wandered a bit when the scenery was smitten by lush green fields and clear waters... The romance of railway travel has captivated many. Together with the elements of adventure, nostalgia, and the scenic beauty of landscapes rolling by, there is something inherently romantic about the rhythmic wheels on tracks. Furthermore, the physical act of traversing distances by train mirrors the metaphorical journey of life itself, complete with its twists and turns. Just as the train navigates through tunnels, individuals encounter obstacles, setbacks, and moments of uncertainty along their own paths of life.

As the journey progressed, I started admiring the train more. It felt like a train of thoughts. There was a family seated across, full of energetic talk and laugh. A couple of times, one of the small boys came over and peeped into my laptop, made some funny faces and left...Suddenly I was reminded of my son's mischiefs, I chuckled inside. I was immersed in the preparation for my conference, when the TTE came; I jolted. He calmly addressed me by my full name, confirmed my ID proof and never asked me for the ticket. Perhaps, the entire system of train services has changed. I resumed my work again. I ordered my food via Food OnTrack App. It was delivered to me at the next station. To my utter disbelief I was happy to receive freshly prepared meals but reminisced about the times when I travelled with my parents and grandparents as a child...

Most often we travelled as a family for attending a wedding or for pilgrimage purposes. My mother used to pack lunch and snacks for everyone to munch along the way. We used to talk, laugh, play games and have fun together as a family. But now all are glued to smart phones. Nobody has time to appreciate the simple joys of life. Suddenly I was jolted by my co-worker's call, informing me the details and location of the conference venue. The two nights that I spend on the train was very peaceful and chilling. A slight drizzle led me to an unfamiliar territory. When I reached my destination – Delhi station, it was extremely crowded. Even I tried to save an old lady who accidently tripped over the escalator...not to mention being a hero. Later I booked a cab and left for the conference immediately.

In essence, train travel is a catalyst for self-discovery. Through the rhythm of the rails, the beauty of the landscapes, and the connections forged along the way, individuals embark on a journey of the soul, with a deeper understanding of themselves and the world around them. This journey allowed me to reconnect with myself. As the train carriages traverse landscapes both familiar and unfamiliar, are afforded the chance to sift through the complexities of our thoughts, confront our fears, and envision new possibilities for the future. As we journey through life, let us remember the timeless appeal of train travel and the profound connections it fosters between people and places.

CHAPTER FOURTEEN

Journeying Through Time: Tracks of Memory

Beena Anil

Nostalgic when I see a train
A train of memories trails my mind
Tracking the past with sweet memories
Of my childhood days to adulthood days
Excitement was the key to be on her with a valid ticket
Knowing when my journey ends

Train journey is a tapestry of emotion, thrill, reflection, memory and encounters for a woman like me with great dreams. I immerse in an oscillating experience to entwine hearts and souls. Whistles and rhythmic clack of wheels echo my days of melodies. Single or double or more, my travel promises the horizon of hope with no dismay. The richness of train experience enlivens my past in the present to have a glorious future. My childhood journey on train ensembles the mark of diverse lives with a glimpse of challenges and promises to recollect innocence and memories to make as well as keep. My train journey has transformed the hustle bustle life with myriad hues to introspect childhood romantic adventures for personal triumph. That long silent journey on the long tracks transformed my power to embrace resilience gracefully. From fighting for the window seat to swapping stories with co-passengers was the camaraderie of the train journey of the past. One could find curiosity in my eyes with a sense of wonder to see the moving mountains, bustling stations, flying trees in a jiffy but with gripping senses. All OTHERS travelled in the compartment with great smiles and humility while sharing stories or food to denote our Indian culture and tradition. Today's summer vacation is not for carefree time of leisure but filled with responsibilities and academic developments. For many, vacation is all about study schedules, courses, assignments, assessments. As a child, embarking on an annual pilgrimage to my grandmother's house with my sister was filled with warm memories. The 150 years old house welcomed us with a vibrant smile of our grandma and the house was always filled with laughter and the house seemed to hold my memories of my childhood. Homemade traditional food, boundless bounding of kinship, cracking jokes, intergenerational thoughts, and the power of familial connections always engulfed aside of chirping birds, serenity and serendipity. Climbing trees without being mindful of gravity had made me a fearless explorer, who could traverse the road not taken with unseen hopes of sanguinity. Playing hide and seek and chasing games with cousins in the sun dappled lush green backyard garden, grandparents sharing anecdotes with their life experiences which forged me to understand that familial bonds could be rewired with beautiful memories. After a month's stay getting back to hustle bustle life had manifested a profound sense of gratitude for the purposeful existence. Today, my children have a different notion of vacation, I understand that though their summer vacation is unconventional but they can emerge stronger, wiser and smarter to overcome challenges in life and their vacation is undeniably (like mine) rewarding as it is the period for self-growth and self-discovery.

In the world of AI, travelling is faster with Wi-Fi connectivity and an array of amenities with no paper, less queues and no physical people. Lots of benefits in this era, but Journeys lost their sheen due to human dis-connectivity of sharing and caring. The Aradhana movie song 'mere sapnon ki rani' is the all-time favorite across ages.

The cutting edge technology won't mar the interest of train with the click-clack rhythmic sound with the heartbeat of happiness and rejuvenation.

Train is the lifeline to many, I guess, especially to the renowned film director Mr.Mani Rathnam, as most of his films have train as a mode of symbol and metaphor. People connect with train for business, romance, education, profession and daily life. Southern Railways has given a sense of freedom to many by breaking barriers of fear and frustration. The railway platforms housed many to feel the sense of pride after tasting the fruit of success though many unsuccessful stories were turned into symbols of struggle. Travelling in a second class was an experience to be with nature, the feather rough touch of wind made me breath less but capturing the shots with my eyes were in my memory till my next journey. Today travelling in an AC compartment diminishes my memories of the journey but I rekindle the past journey with great freshness and agility.

CHAPTER FIFTEEN

Love Stories and Train Tracks in Bollywood : Where Destinies Meet

Sonika Sheoran

Trains have always been a part of Indian cinema, be it lovers parting from each other or a nation dividing into two. Train stations are places where people express their deep emotions before saying a final goodbye and give a big hug to each other when they meet after a long time.

From films like *Gadar* (2001) to *Laapataa ladies (2023)*, Indian directors have always found a way to show trains more than a mode of transportation. Gadar is a film directed by Anil sharma in 2001. It is a story based on the partition of India where the natives were forced to choose between two parts of India. Now, at that time, during the 1947, trains were the major transportation vehicles and train stations have seen more dead bodies than hospitals. In the starting scenes of the film Gadar, people were searching for their family members among the bodies lying on the floor, some were running here and there in hope of finding their relatives. *Laapataa Ladies* is based on 2001, a film where two newly wedded brides who were wearing the same dress that is red saree and dupatta get exchanged with each other.

An important change occurred when the railway system was introduced to India in the middle of the 19th century. Trains promoted trade and urbanisation by making it easier for people and goods to travel over great distances. Indian cinema immediately responded to this newfound freedom. The amazing spectacle of trains was captured in early films, many of which were influenced by documentary styles. These films emphasised the importance of trains in connecting remote parts of the country. With the development of Indian cinema, trains came to represent social mobility, representing characters leaving their villages in pursuit of better jobs.

education or lives.

In Indian cinema, railway stations have taken on significant emotional roles beyond their practical use. These stations, teeming with activity, hope, and despair, are microcosms of Indian society. The platform turns into a stage where people say goodbye to loved ones inconsolably and set out on journeys burdened with their goals and aspirations. This trope is best shown in movies like "Dilwale Dulhania Le Jayenge," (1995) where the memorable train station scene has come to represent the movie's enduring romance. On the other hand, reunions at the station, which signify the end of protracted separations and the happiness of being reunited with loved

ones, are equally heartbreaking. The horrific episode of India's 1947 partition has always been etched in the collective memory of the country. Trains, which carried millions of people across recently drawn borders, ended up being the unwitting witnesses to this mass displacement. Movies such as "Gadar: Ek Prem Katha" employ the visuals of crammed trains carrying refugees to illustrate the human cost of division. In the terrifying station scene that opens the movie, people are frantically looking through the bodies scattered across the platform for loved ones. This graphic metaphor powerfully brings to light the tragedy and violence that transpired during the partition. Here, the train takes on symbolic

meaning related to forced migration,
homeland loss, and displacement. Train travel is a common lens through which to examine the experiences of women in Indian society. The train is portrayed in films like *'Mother India'* (1975) as a means of escape that gives women the opportunity to overcome social constraints. On the other hand, trains can also stand for the restrictions placed on women's freedom of movement. In the film *"Laapataa Ladies,"* the inadvertent switching of two recently weds during a train ride underscores the social control exerted over a woman's identity and freedom of movement within the constraints of traditional red attire and marriage. The train ride turns
into a place of both confusion and potential liberation, making the women face their predetermined roles. The train's unrelenting motion represents life itself, which is a never-ending journey with its ups and downs and arrivals and departures. Trains are a metaphor for time passing, bringing characters forward into new experiences and making them face their pasts. The endless length of the tracks symbolises the boundless possibilities of life, while the steady clatter of the wheels can be seen as the unrelenting march of time.

With the development of Indian film, trains have been a steady companion over the years. When filmmakers are attempting to investigate the social, cultural, and emotional landscapes of India, they continue to be a potent instrument in their hands. Trains are powerful symbols that have a profound impact on Indian audiences, since they may represent everything from the aspiration of a fresh start to the agony of being uprooted against one's will. It is probable that the train will continue to play a prominent role in the Indian film industry as it continues to develop. This is because the train is able to capture the energy and complexity of a nation that is always moving.

CHAPTER SIXTEEN

Terrible to 'Train'able

Leena.P

"The most beautiful emotion we can experience is the mystical" –
Albert Einstein

O train, my Mangalore Mail,
Pick me up from human ocean pile.
My mom never made reservations
It only worsened my fear of suffocation.
We merely got places to stand
With the support of porter's brawn.
She thought it was waste of money
Would ever utter 'Sure, next time, honey'.
I never knew she saved how much
As it is impossible to keep in touch.
Some goodbyes came early in my life,
Completely forgot what it was like
Having a mom and a dad still alive.
Will I ever feel it again?
Not the pain but the align
Love and Life gone by.
I marry the man of my choice,
Tables turn – I travel only in AC coach.
Every ride you being my 'berth' mother
Nursing me, carrying me like no other.

Fourteen hours of journey inside you
Deport me from one realm to another
Dark side of my life with tether
Slipping into so much brighter
Grandparents' blessings, kisses and hugs tighter.
Sitting near the window, how nice
To see all my worries vanish.
Smooth sailing, people-watching
My ride is always mind-blowing.
You remind me to hold on to happiness
As though I agree never to stuck with sadness.
Some unheard stories, some unseen relations,
Quick yet so thrilling,
Mystical yet so real
With a smile on my lips to enjoy the trail.
O train, my Mangalore Mail,
Pick me up from human ocean pile.

CHAPTER SEVENTEEN

Phoenix on a Night Express

Ardra Ann Thomas

Dusk surged in its faint glow,
  Tainting the carriage in crimson hues.
  Boarded she in it, with a heart full of thoughts.
  Leaving behind the remnants of a life,
  Where venomous whispers devoured her.
  Passing the golden fields and silver rivers,
  Gloom loomed into her indigo-patched face.
  With each mile, shed she a tear,
  Weighed by her haunting memories.
  But the sobs sank in the rhythmic clatters.
  Slipped hours silently from her gaze,
  Piercing the arch of the sky in its magical bloom.
  Scars, once raw and unyielding,
  That etched her soul slowly and steadily
  Transformed into marks of resilience.
  As the night falls, darkness of pain swells up,
  Again, for one last chance to gulp her.
  A ghost of her former existence, and
  The scarlet memories of her woes,
  Put forth an ultimate silent outbreak.

Stoic silence ensnared her face and thoughts.
Through the moonlit valleys and starlit cities,
Travelled she that entire night with eyes open.
Scattering her burdened past freely,
And carelessly like dandelions in spring.
With the misty dawn, adorned she a new robe.
The wheels click and clatter - clack, clack.
With every breath, echoing her heartbeats
Filled with a cadence of courage and warmth,
Flowed, she slowly to a future uncharted.
With the past a distant, faint shadow,
The train's hum proclaimed a melody of freedom.
Each turn a note, each stretch a chord.
Creating a symphony of revival and rebirth
Like the spirit of a phoenix - indestructible.
The whistle wailed, piercing the morning's ears
To a platform of new life and new self.
Looked, she one last time at the glass windows
That reflected her face with glorious hues.
Realisation dawned: she is me, and I am her.

CHAPTER EIGHTEEN

Then and Now

Himanshu Kumar

Sitting at my desk doodling
Restlessly
Waiting to see the needle weave magic —
unseen, unsung, unheard
Trains of thoughts whistled by
one by one
at full throttle
without unloading their freight
I signalled the drivers to stop
but in vain
None valued my desperation
"How insensitive Muses are!"
I jumped onto a wagon
seeking to grab an idea
through daredevilry
but ended up
biting the dust
literally and metaphorically.
I red flagged the trains,
Lied on the tracks
with racing heart and bounding pulse
Realising little that they had diverted

from the path painstakingly drawn by me
"Have patience, idiot", I heard.
My spirits sank
A little idea is what I craved for—
one little idea!
For my first venture—
my inaugural poem.
Sitting at my desk doodling
Patiently
Having seen the Earth pirouette tirelessly
for years
I shouted, "Next!".
He entered my mind,
jostling his way through
a sea of wannabes.
All decked up, he struggled
with my questions
while there was clamour outside.
Suddenly, with a thud,
a dozen candidates came in
almost falling over each other
partly embarrassed, partly confused.
I looked up and remarked—
"Wait for your turn,
For patience is a virtue"
They left the room hurriedly
To queue up outside
like ants.
I stole a glance at my anthologies
placed neatly on a shelf
And smiled to myself.

Essay on Mobility and Space(s) creating Gendered Borders in Local Train

Suparna Roy

The visual sense of trains showcases mobility, and also offers a space that covers and secures the identities explicitly. Talking on Gender, as the term suggest, is just not between man and a woman, rather it refers to all identities struggling within the spectrum of gender spaces. The term 'Matribhumi' draws its origin from a Malayalam newspaper titled the same, which meant motherland. The debate this term draws is how much is this gendered space validated equally. Gendered spaces on trains typically refer to designated areas or compartments separated by gender, commonly found in certain cultures or regions. These segregated spaces aim to provide comfort, safety, and privacy for passengers, particularly women. The effectiveness and appropriateness of gender-segregated spaces on trains have been subject to debate. While some argue that these measures are necessary to protect women from harassment and ensure their safety, others view them as reinforcing gender stereotypes and limiting women's freedom of movement. The provision of gendered spaces on trains reflects broader social attitudes towards gender roles, safety concerns, and cultural norms in different parts of the world.

The female commuters in West Bengal local trains face such egregious forms of sexual violence and harassment. The experiences often narrated details a pervasive issue of gender-based violence that robs women of their sense of safety and dignity in public spaces. The public domain and private allowance, where the diabolic power play of public/private function as has been a historical issue of complex patriarchal regimes, and as Phadke, Shilpa and Sameera in one of their article writes: So long as women's presence in public space continues to be framed within the binary of public/private and within the complexity layered hierarchies of class, community, and gender, an unconditional right to public space will remain a fantasy (2009, 186). Addressing this problem requires a multi-faceted approach involving education, cultural shifts, and robust enforcement of laws to protect women's rights and safety. Providing safe transportation options, increasing police presence, and implementing awareness campaigns to challenge harmful attitudes and behaviors are all important steps toward creating a more inclusive and secure environment for women. On August 24, 2015, a large group of men launched a violent assault on female passengers aboard the Matribhumi train. These men, displaying their masculinity without reservation, expressed their determination to halt the operation of the Matribhumi train. They obstructed the train's route in North 24 Parganas district, entering the coaches to verbally and physically abuse the women onboard. Many of the women sought refuge by hiding under their seats, while some even sought safety beneath the train on the railway track. This attack followed a series of prior blockades and threats from angered men demanding the discontinuation of the Matribhumi train service. The violence extended beyond just the female passengers of the Matribhumi train, affecting anyone in the vicinity of the train, including women on other trains, on the platform, and in nearby streets.

In the context of "Matribhumi local" and "A Force Gendered Creation in Public Mobility," we delve into the intersection of local transportation infrastructure and gender dynamics, particularly within the framework of a region or community that values its maternal heritage. In Matribhumi, or 'Motherland,' local transportation systems play a pivotal role in shaping daily life and societal interactions. However, historically, these systems have often overlooked the diverse needs and safety concerns of different genders. "A Force Gendered Creation in Public Mobility" emphasizes the imperative to design transportation infrastructure with a nuanced understanding of gender dynamics. To address this, Matribhumi's approach to public mobility embraces inclusivity and equity, recognizing that women, men, and gender-diverse individuals may have distinct requirements and experiences when navigating urban spaces. Safety emerges as a paramount concern, prompting the implementation of measures such as well-lit pathways, surveillance systems, and gender-sensitive design features to foster a secure environment for all users, particularly women and marginalized groups. Moreover, Matribhumi's transportation planners prioritize accessibility, recognizing the varied travel patterns shaped by caregiving responsibilities, economic constraints, and societal norms. This entails ensuring that public transit is not only physically accessible but also financially viable and convenient for everyone, irrespective of gender identity or socioeconomic status.

In a Matribhumi context, the notion of "force gendered creation" underscores the deliberate integration of gender perspectives into every stage of transportation planning and development. This involves consulting diverse stakeholders, including women's groups, gender activists, and community leaders, to co-create solutions that address the unique mobility needs and aspirations of all residents. By embracing a force gendered approach to public mobility, Matribhumi aims to foster an inclusive and empowering urban environment where transportation systems not only facilitate movement but also reflect and reinforce the principles of gender equality, social justice, and maternal heritage. Through collaborative efforts and ongoing dialogue, Matribhumi endeavors to set a precedent for gender-sensitive urban planning and inspire similar initiatives worldwide.

The creation of women-only compartments in local mobility systems can indeed be a contentious topic, as it can perpetuate gender binaries and may not address the root causes of safety concerns or gender-based harassment. While these compartments are often introduced with the intention of providing a safer space for women, they can inadvertently reinforce the idea that women need separate, segregated spaces for protection. This approach can further entrench gender stereotypes and fail to address the underlying issues of harassment and gender-based violence that affect public transportation. Moreover, women-only compartments may not be a viable solution for everyone. They can be restrictive for individuals who do not conform to traditional gender norms or who may feel safer in mixed-gender spaces. Additionally, they may not address the safety concerns of women outside of designated compartments, leaving them vulnerable in other parts of the transportation system.

Instead of relying solely on women-only compartments, it's essential to adopt a more holistic approach to improving safety and inclusivity in local mobility systems.

- Enhanced Security: Augmenting the presence of security personnel and deploying surveillance cameras throughout transportation hubs and vehicles can serve as effective deterrents against harassment, ensuring the safety of all passengers.
- Education and Awareness: Launching campaigns aimed at raising awareness about respectful behavior and encouraging bystander intervention can cultivate a culture of accountability and solidarity among commuters, fostering a more supportive and protective atmosphere for everyone.

- Community Engagement: Actively involving local communities, including women's groups and marginalized populations, in decision-making processes enables a deeper understanding of their unique needs and concerns. This engagement facilitates the development of more tailored and effective solutions to address safety issues.
- Designing for Inclusivity: Creating transportation spaces that prioritize inclusivity involves designing well-lit, accessible, and universally accommodating environments. By considering the diverse needs of all passengers, regardless of gender, these spaces can contribute to a more welcoming and secure atmosphere for everyone to navigate.

The introduction of women-only compartments in local trains can indeed present challenges for transgender individuals, as it may contribute to their exclusion and marginalization within public transportation systems. Firstly, the binary nature of women-only compartments inherently excludes transgender individuals who may not identify strictly as male or female. This exclusion perpetuates societal norms that dictate gender based on physical characteristics, disregarding the diverse identities and experiences of transgender people. Furthermore, the enforcement of gender-specific compartments can subject transgender individuals to discrimination and harassment when attempting to access these spaces. Transgender individuals may face verbal abuse, physical violence, or denial of entry, as their presence challenges traditional notions of gender segregation within public transportation. Additionally, the lack of inclusive policies and awareness training among transportation staff exacerbates the difficulties faced by transgender passengers. Without adequate support mechanisms in place, transgender individuals may feel unsafe or unwelcome when navigating public transportation, further isolating them from essential mobility services.

Moreover, the existence of women-only compartments may reinforce harmful stereotypes and stigmatize transgender individuals as potential threats or disruptors of gender-segregated spaces. This portrayal perpetuates misconceptions about transgender people and contributes to their social exclusion and marginalization within society. In conclusion, while women-only compartments in local trains aim to address safety concerns for women passengers, they inadvertently perpetuate discrimination and exclusion against transgender individuals. Addressing these challenges requires a comprehensive approach that prioritizes inclusivity, awareness, and sensitivity training within public transportation systems, ensuring that all passengers, regardless of gender identity, can access and utilize services without fear of discrimination or harassment.

CHAPTER TWENTY

Train of Thoughts...

Reema Sara Benson

I don't often travel by train, but very recently I got an opportunity to travel from Kottayam to the capital city of Kerala, Thiruvananthapuram. The journey was indeed a very tedious and long journey which comprises of meeting new people and lot of sightseeing I've always thought that having a companion on a lengthy trip makes it more thrilling. And train travel has always been a prime example to that.

A couple of months ago, I travelled from Kottayam to Ernakulam with a friend of mine. The journey started with just the two of us knowing each other but as we reached the our station we met and talked to almost everyone in our nearby seats. It is always a very exhilarating experience to get to know a complete stranger life story and their interests. Some stories leave us wishing for more, some cause us to reflect on our own behaviour, while others impart valuable life lessons.

One of the people I remember meeting in my journey was Nandana, a single mother to a 10yr old who was travelling to Chennai for her new job. She is one of the resilient people I have, met up until recently. She is a person who had to go through plan A, B, C to finally reach her destination. She taught me keep looking for what we are searching, even when the entire world is against you. She is also a very chatty person which kept me interested in the entire five-hour ride. Thank you Nandana chechy for being an idol of hope and perseverance.

Further on the sceneries that flash through the window gives us unique perspective on how we see life. Passing through Varkala Sivagiri station helped me understand the various household around the popular tourist area. I observed animals and people coexisting in a dilapidated shed. Run-down homes that are nearly falling apart, sewage drains clogged with trash and train crap, etc. However, I know that despite all of these challenges, the residents went on with their lives.

During one of the train trips, I experienced the most intriguing event. I met a young lady who was going to Kannur from Kottayam. Although I can't remember her name, she asked me a question before we parted that has since become a treasured aspect of my life: "Tell me anything you have done, or wish to do, that you believe I should do? It can be anything you want it to be, easy or difficult. I swear I will finish it as long as you give me the rest of my life to do it. Though I couldn't figure out why, I gave it some thought and advised her to "make at least one person smile every day." and she asked me if I would like a challenge as well and I told her I did "tell the 5 people I hated the most, that I love them and respect them". Though it was difficult, I agreed to it, and we said our goodbyes.

Mostly I don't remember the people and conversations I had but this one always stays fresh in my mind because each time I talk to those five people I think about her and that day. I don't want to just have experience and then let them go. I want to remember these meetings and embrace the fact that they happened. So, whenever I leave someone who has left an amazing impact in my life, I ask them to give me a challenge. I never saw that lady ever again but what I do know is that she gave me a gift that never once stopped giving.

Finally, I believe that trains are often related to as a journey of life. The way the wind blows our hair, TC's coming around to check the comfort of the passengers, smiles exchanged among strangers, different snack vendors selling snacks and drinks, rhythm of the wheels on the track. They often teach us various aspects of life.

CHAPTER TWENTY-ONE

Next Janam

Sujarani Mathew

"Take care my dear, call me as soon as you get there!"

"Yeah mom, sure...sure." The engine clanked and the whistle hooted. The train slowly began to chug it's way." Take care Priya...", her mom's voice was strangely insistent.

"Yes mother, bye. I will call"- ' if I remember when I get there' thought Priya as she took her seat in the compartment. She quickly kicked her meagre luggage under the seats and prepared to make herself comfy, when she saw the only other passenger in the compartment- a young and ...'well, personable guy', she thought, who was lazily observing her. Sighting her looking at him, he smiled "Hi"

"Hello" replied Priya and hastily grabbed a text she always carried during such journeys to ward off unnecessary male attention. Retreating towards a window seat, she sat back opening her book and appeared to bury herself in the book

Minutes passed by. Priya was soon getting bored with the book she had read thrice already. Making a quick introspection, she smiled at her own behaviour. Generally, she did not find it difficult to converse with strangers in the train to while the time by...'why was she hesitant this time? Cause the co- passenger was young? Or because of the reason that there was no one else around?'

' Well, there seems to be no one getting into the compartment inspite of two or three more stations going by. Better chat with him- or I will be bored to death'. Priya shut her book and pretended to look out and admire the scenery for some time. Looking around she appeared to see the young man for the first time and asked, "Where are you bound?"

"Ernakulam"

"Oh!" replied Priya

" You? " He queried back.

" Me too." ' That means we would have to spend twenty-four hours together having the same destination,' thought Priya.

Desultory conversation followed with the usual Indian enquiries on personal information, family and friends. Srikanth learned that she was working with an NGO and of a good Christian family with impeccable background and Priya realised that he was at the time a lecturer in Karnataka University having completed his MTech and also of a respectable Hindu tradition.

"I didn't know people with MTech taught in Universities- I thought they worked in MNCs - what do you teach?"

"My post is as a Lecturer in Fibre Optics. And yeah, I just took it up for fun. It's the only one post for that stream there. I am thinking of changing my job. That's why I am going to Ernakulam- to attend an interview - with a Holland company."

"Well, hope you get the job." quipped Priya. " Yeah, me too. It's the first time I am going to Ernakulam. Let's see if the journey turns lucky for me," smiled Srikanth.

"You will surely get it," said Priya and instantly wondered why she was so sure for him. 'Who was he of hers??' Srikanth quickly looked up at her and noticing her confusion said hastily, "Thanks, for your good heart." Priya breathed a sigh of relief, and graded him mentally 'Not a bad person - in fact, quite a gentleman!'

Silence ensued for some time, only for Srikanth to break it- " You often go to Ernakulam?"

"Well, I am working with *Anweshi* there"

"And your mother always sees you off?"

"Mostly, why?"

"She seems so very...err..protective"

"That's how all mothers are, " defended Priya

"Yeah, I guess...your mother seemed so scared to let her pretty daughter go off with one bad villain with her in the room..." smiled Srikanth reminiscing.

'Pretty??' the word hung in Priya 's ears...she had often heard herself described so and always ignored it as not important. But to hear it from this young man's lips felt ...well, felt good. "Comeon, it's nothing like that," she said aloud "she knows her daughter knows to toe the line"

"The line?"

" Yeah, the line that mothers of respectable families give their daughters who have to study abroad- Love marriage is fine, but as long as he is of a good character, appearance, with a good job and of the same community." Priya explained.

Srikanth whistled "Tall order"

"It's all for their children's best" Priya's comment was philosophic.

The train whistled nearing a tunnel. The sudden darkness and the deafening noise of the train going through the tunnel kept them silent for some time. "Tell me, do you really think there is much difference between religions?" Srikanth wanted to know.

" Well, I guess, there is a lot of difference culturally...and in some beliefs"- " what do you think is the plus point in Hindu belief from other religions?" Priya continued wishing to change the track of the conversation.

"Plus point? well, for me I think it's our belief in reincarnation. You have a chance to live again, next *Janam*."

"That's a good idea, having a second chance..."agreed Priya

"Even if your life doesn't turn out the way you want, you can have the consolation that there could be another time... Srikanth said slowly..."even if I don't get this job...maybe next time"

It was soon gathering dusk and the train began to slow down for the next station. "I wonder if there would be someone to get in at the station. This compartment has been empty for such a long time." said Priya. Standing up to reach his bag, Srikanth said, "Empty?? What a jab to my male ego!"

Priya laughed, " You don't look like the kind to get your male ego deflated that easily."

"Really, now what's the reason for that? " quipped Srikanth flexing his muscles and grinning impishly down at her.

Laughing at him, Priya had to fight hard to ignore the strange tug at her heart. "Did religion really matter, she wondered.... Srikanth really scored high in all other of her mother's criteria...' 'Don't be silly', she admonished herself and pushed the thought away.

The train pulled up at the next station and someone climbed in. He came into the compartment with a number of baggage and started depositing it everywhere. Straightening up, he looked at his fellow passengers and grinned "Hi, where are you both to? Ernakulam? so am I. By the way, I am Vivek, when do you think we will reach there?" He went into a friendly chat with the two youngsters.

After sometime he asked "so you are cousins or something?"

"Cousins? No..."said Srikanth

"Oh, old friends then", concluded Vivek. " Well, as a matter of fact, we just got to know each other on this train," said Priya.

" Seriously!!? Uh,oh..." Vivek was silent for sometime. "Happy to make your acquaintance anyway," he rejoined. They went on chatting until each one turned to their bunks to sleep.

The next day morning saw the compartment full of passengers, all bound for one or the other destination. Priya heard someone say soon after she got up: "One more hour for Ernakulam. " Really, then I must get ready," said Vivek and began getting all his parcels out, characteristically of him.

" Morning Priya, "Srikanth entered with two paper cups." Which do you prefer - tea or coffee?"

" Coffee," said she promptly. "Good, I got coffee for you too. Here.."

"There was no need for you to bother..." began Priya

"Don't be silly- drink it"

Priya wondered whether she should dislike his obvious peremptoriness. She decided to let it go and reached for the coffee.

Glancing through the newspapers Srikanth said, "You get down at Ernakulam North, don't you? That is just in half an hour. I will have to wait some more to get down at South, my station."

" Oh, I also get down South," said Priya.

" South?" Srikanth looked up.

"Well, I could go both ways," Priya's voice was defensive.

"Of course," said Srikanth looking down at his newspaper.

' What is wrong with me?' Priya chided herself. 'I ought to get down at the North station. Why am I doing this? Some questions do not have any answers...'she told herself.

Vivek got up when Ernakulam North neared and began to push his luggage out. But on the way he hugged Srikanth and said, "Let's have a selfie, buddy...great to get to know you people." Come on Priya, join in," said Srikanth. "What of your contact numbers?" asked Vivek. "I have yours, will give u a ring right now. What of your number, Priya?" said Srikanth. There was a pause, "Sorry, I don't share my number with all" Priya felt that there was a bug in her throat. She turned away chiding herself under Srikanth's gaze.

The train whistled on...South station came up. The two youngsters got down and walked towards the exit. Priya tried to make casual conversation, but somehow the words got stuck.

Srikanth too was mute. They stopped at the gate - two strangers who met to part. "Well. Best wishes for your interview," said Priya, and hoped her smile was bright.

" Yeah, and well...bye for now I guess...until we meet next *Janam*, right? " Srikanth quirked his lips into a smile.

" Ok, bye," Priya beat a hasty retreat. 'No, don't look back, don't look back' - one moment's madness could be a lifetime's folly - she reminded herself of her mother's words as she walked away.

'Priya, turn around just once...' Srikanth murmured to himself. But he was discouraged by the figure of Priya plodding away looking straight ahead. '*Paladke dekh* Priya...'Srikanth said, clenching his fingers in despair. Priya was having a battle between her head and her heart. 'Oh, I can't help it...' Priya turned around unable to stop herself any longer--in time to see him turn away, disappointed. Priya saw Srikanth squaring his shoulders and heave his bag onto it and walk away... slowly, very slowly.

Two weeks later at home, as she flipped through the newspaper Priya's attention was riveted onto a job advertisement - 'Inviting applicants to the post of Lecturer in Applied Physics and Instrumentation, specialized in Fibre Optics, Karnataka University."

" Best wishes Srikanth, in your new job... with all my heart" she murmured.

" Priya, do come to the kitchen...I need your help", called her mother.

" Yes mom, I am coming... "

CHAPTER TWENTY-TWO

Train as a symbol of connection and separation

Durdanah Masoodi

I had never experienced the essence of a train journey in 20 years. Its symbolic importance, what can journey tell you apart from the fact that you are traveling in those consecutive square boxes. As long as I did not sit in one of the compartments of those boxes, it was one more mode of transport for me, nothing else. As a student, I left my place in May 2018 for the first time, and that was for admission purposes in New Delhi. I along with my father boarded a train to New Delhi, while the train was moving, we knew it was going to take us that entire night to reach Delhi, so a lot was crossing my mind. Besides, there was a lot that I could see that a flight journey would not have allowed me to experience.

This a gentle reminder that till that time it was just a means of transport, I had no idea that a few train journeys would be cherished by me lifelong for exposing me to both jolly and sad moments. It is not just about moments, but about that transformation and lens through which I would see train and train journeys ahead in my life. As far as visualizing my surroundings I could see a crowd of people, a cacophony that pierced my ears, some messy washrooms, light food stalls, heavy trollies, mothers carrying trollies and crying babies along, and those high-pitched social and political discussions. Besides, I don't know what it was in that journey, but to some extent, my mind was penetrated with this feeling of 'leaving.' I started realizing I had left my place, family, and dear ones, for something more. So in short, I started missing home. But back in my mind, I knew that was just the admission formality time, and joining was in July, which meant I had to be back home for some more duration. This was an impermanent moment, but a lasting visualization. Finally, after I was done with all the formalities, we left back home. The month of June passed with all the necessary preparations such as borrowing certain things, documentation work, and a lot more. And in a jiffy, July said, Hi.

It was mid-July, and we booked the train again. This time my mother planned to accompany me, and deep down in my heart I knew it was going to be a very perplexing journey for me. On one side I had this excitement and curiosity to land in India's number one college for 6 years now (Miranda House), but on the other hand, being extremely close to my mother, and bidding her adieu was going to be heart-wrenching for me. We had reserved a compartment for three of us, my parents sat on one side and I on the opposite side. The entire journey filled my mind with perplexing emotions. It was not just the face of my parents constantly in front of me, but it was the smell of their existence, and in short, I started missing them a lot on the train only. At least at that time, they were in front of me, but I knew within a few days they would return home as well, and I would have to start the struggling journey in Delhi on my own.

To be quite clear, platforms/airports and I are incompatible partners. But there is a new perspective. Whenever I leave 'for' home, then I find platforms a sight of relief and relaxation. But whenever I leave 'from' home then nothing is as suffocating as that moment which I have to spend till the train departs. While the earlier condition extends the emotion of 'connection' for me, the latter extends nothing but 'Profound separation.' Meanwhile, we reached Delhi, and I finally joined college. Tough I would say was the part when my parents left for home, and again it was this 'platform' that gave rise to all the needed emotions. Life kept on moving, and in my independent attained capacity, I was struggling to get adjusted to this new cosmopolitan city. Nevertheless, with time some blessed people started making the place comfortable, and that is how Delhi and I began a familiar journey.

Platforms became the new normal of my travel life, from one metro station to the other, that is what engaged me in Delhi apart from my academics. Now platforms extended a guiding hand to me, willing to show me around Delhi. I readily accepted the offer. For a period, they were not about 'connection' or 'separation' but 'ultimate excitement' to explore more. Quite a long time had passed, mid-semester breaks, short winter breaks, and long summer breaks began approaching. And these breaks became a catalyst for those temporarily untouched emotions of connection and separation. Almost our every break except for one, was sent at home. However this time there was a slight difference in the set of people accompanying me. They were my friends, and ah, everyone juggling with the same emotions as I did. We always approached platforms with a thrill, we started packing a week before, and such was our excitement to be home. But every time our return was a pain. Our meets at the platform lacked enthusiasm and thrill, packings were done at the last moment, and faces reflected every ounce of inner situation. Meanwhile, this to and fro kept happening yearly, and we found ourselves its ultimate target every time it approached us. Time passed, the end of the degree came closer, and guess what, a new transformation.

This time when everyone had to be home, it was no longer just a 'thrill,' but remember what I mentioned earlier, a set of 'perplexing' emotions. This happened because friends had become buddies, outings, and hangings with them were a new way to relax, simply, we were going to miss each other, and therefore platforms for us now were on one side connoting that reunion and connection with family, but on the other hand, there was this constant emoticon of 'separation' on all the faces. As close as were we approaching the platform, everyone kept saying, 'We are moving a step ahead to plan meets, which were otherwise instant meets,' 'We are set for long separations and yearned reunions- because to plan reunions at home was going to be a herculean task, as everyone is not available on a decided day, familial engagements, and a lot more.' We all lived in different areas and with a slight smile, everyone boarded at their respective stations. Hands kept waving, and eyes reflected the need of the hour.

Some journeys ended, while others started. Traveling via platforms became a new engaging activity, life brought to that stage where not even a single nerve recognized train/train track or the platform merely as boxes or constructed sites. Life has been successful in achieving one of its objectives- making me realize, cherish, and ponder over every step that I take, go deep into it, and take from it the best possible lesson. Transformation of one sort was achieved while setting the base for the others to come.

CHAPTER TWENTY-THREE

The 'Other' in Theroux's Travelogues

Niborna Hazarika

'Othering' is a much-used term in recent travel writing studies, though confusingly it is often used in two slightly different senses. In a weaker, more generic sense, 'othering' refers to the process through which people of one culture recognize and emphasize the distinctions between themselves and those of another culture. In a strong sense, however, it has come to refer more specifically to the processes and strategies by which one culture depicts another culture as not only different but also inferior to itself.

The travel writers place themselves as an outsider and look at the new place and people as Others in a conscious manner. Paul Theroux has traveled to many places around the world on trains. While travelling through various places he notices the differences between his own American self and the people of different countries. Based on this contrast he has created the concept of Othering.

Travel literature tends to have an exclusive concentration on the Self, an emphasis on empirical detail, and a linear progression across time and space. Travel writers often describe the 'other' in negative terms. They distinguish the manners and customs of the Other from their country and consider the Other as inferior.

The ideological components of travel writing, and the wider rhetorical purposes served by the frequent inclination of travel writers to frame other groups and cultures in an antagonistic or contemptuous fashion, are subject matters that have been concentrated heavily in the most recent flurry of travel literature. In particular, these are issues that have focused their attention especially on the depictions of other people and places offered in Western travel writing, and in Western culture more generally.

The Other functions as the Self's polar antithesis. It helps in the conceptualization of the Self. The Other is looked upon as fragile, incompetent, easily duped, and prone to immortality. The image of the Other is produced as inferior.

Travel writers discriminate between the familiar surroundings at home and the traveling destination. This is shown by the production of difference. It is done to cater to the interests of the readers. The travel writer constructs the idea of the Other to bring forth the distinction in question.

Travel writing is affected by colonialism. The culture of the imperial countries is presented as supreme and more practical. The image of the Other reassures the imperial readers not only of superiority over the rest of the world but also of their moral right to that sense of superiority.

In the neo-colonial as in the colonial era, positive as well as negative representations of the Other may work to sustain the unequal power relations between the West and the rest of the world. Other people and other places can in a sense be held hostage by the iconography that attaches to them in Western culture. Much of contemporary travel writing arguably colludes with the tendency in so far as it works first to establish this iconography, and thereafter to underplay the impact of modernity, and especially of tourism, on many other regions of the world.

Moreover, the Other is always seen as exotic, and strange. Exoticism is one of the forms of creating geographical otherness. Whatever constitutes the other is seen with awe and is considered abnormal. Exoticism is visible in the description of the landscape and people and their cultures. In reality, no place is exotic. It is merely a construction by the Self to define the Other. It is used to mystify the Other and create a difference between the two.

The geographical Other can be presented through the picture of Britain. 1882 was the summer of the Falklands War. Britain won the Falklands War against Argentina. They gained supremacy over the world. One Western country looks at another Western country as the Other. One country considers itself to be superior compared to the other country. They look at the other country as exotic, strange, and unusual.

Again, the mode of travel can also be a place of Othering. Whether it is an airplane, a train, or a bus, people of different cultures, castes, and classes travel together within the same means. It is the place where multiple cultures meet. The place becomes multicultural.

There is a world created within the mode itself and the travel writer considers this place as an area to create the concept of Other. He meets various people while traveling together by the same means. He observes them carefully, talks to them, notices their dressing style, looks at their food habits; and based on these observations, he shows them as the Other.

The Other is the inversion of the Self. The travel writers have used the strategies of negation to handle the Other. Travel writing reveals how the dominant cultures of the world produce representations of the other and draw upon contradictions to produce loci from which Western ideologies emerge as superior. Postcolonial theory criticizes these issues delineated in travel narratives.

Most of the travel writers depend on this production to cater to the interests of the readers. To bring forth this difference, the travel writer creates the concept of the 'Other'. This is done for two purposes. One is to make the place and the people of a certain locale look alien to create an aura and then use this concept to create an identity to the Self. According to Edward Said, colonial discourse is hegemonic in nature where the West constructs the imagined

Other. The construction of the Other helps in the conceptualization of the self.

Paul Theroux's *The Great Railway Bazaar: By Train Through Asia* chronicles his four-month journey by train in the year 1973 from London through Europe, the Middle East, the Indian subcontinent, and Southeast Asia and his return via The Trans-Siberian Express. This travelogue demonstrates how he looks at Oriental countries. The people of the Orient countries are described as inferior. The West looks at the Other with disdain and this prejudice against the Other is based on hegemonic control.

The idea of the West being better than the Other is portrayed here. One such instance can be observed in the words of Molesworth. Molesworth, whom Theroux meets while traveling to Istanbul from Paris by The Direct-Orient Express, says from his experience of being in the Indian Army that there are many Indians who so can be treated as absolute equals. They are so well-bred. By talking to them, it is difficult for one to figure out that they are Indians. As Theroux puts it, "he had loved the army and he said that there were many of Indians who were so well bred you could treat them as absolute equals- indeed, talking to them you would hardly know you were talking to Indians" (Theroux 1975: 9). These words by Molesworth indicate that the Indians are considered inferior by the West. Only the well-breed ones can be treated as equal. When he says that by talking to them it is difficult to know that they are Indians indicates that the Indians have a peculiar way of speaking which is different from the rest.

Theroux was comfortable while he was traveling to Paris and was at Calais station. But he said that the great express from Paris turned doubtful and irritating as it reached Istanbul's outskirts. It began to stop at every station to give conductors a chance to fool with notebooks. It became like a Turkish local train. Theroux writes, "The great express from Paris became a doubtful and irritating Turkish locale once it got to Istanbul's outskirts, stopping at every station to give conductors a chance to fool with notebooks in the Turkish Clapham Junctions and Scarsdles" (20). This experience of Theroux shows that the journey in the West is comfortable. But it is not so in the East. Theroux experiences a doubtful and irritating journey in the East.

Hermann whom Theroux met while he was traveling to Amritsar from Lahore paid some extra money to the conductor so that he could travel with a European. He did not want to travel with an Indian because he was afraid that traveling with an Indian might make him face some trouble:

He had bribed the conductor so that he could travel with a European. He didn't want to be in a compartment with an Indian-there might be trouble. (54)

This activity of Hermann indicates that the people of the West consider themselves superior. They do not want to be in the same room with the people of the Other. The Westerners feel that being together with the people of the East might lead them to some trouble. For them, the West is always superior to the Other, over the rest of the world.

In *The Great Railway Bazaar* Theroux looks at the oriental countries as inferior, and low. The people of the Oriental countries are uncivilized and poor. Here he observes things from a Eurocentric perspective. Travel writing is accused of being Eurocentric. It is always the white traveler who travels and defines the Other. This has been discussed by Edward Said in *Orientalism* (1978). The postcolonial theory challenges this purview of looking at things from just the perspective of the white traveler. The white structures his narrative in such a manner as to show that the destinations inhabited by the Orients are not easily accessible or recognizable. It is seen how by the careful use of selected vocabulary and exotic imagery the travel writer mystifies the Other. This is done to prove that the white race is superior. The West always looks at the Other with prejudiced eyes and disdain. The hegemonic control maintained over the Other in socio-political conditions is visible in travel writing too. This makes travel writing a part of colonial discourse.

The Kingdom By The Sea: A Journey Around Great Britain is a written account of a three-month-long journey taken by Paul Theroux around the United Kingdom in the summer of 1982. The travelogue highlights Theroux's way of othering the West though he himself is a Westerner. Theroux takes a detached position and evaluates the English scenario and the problems that trouble the English people and society despite England's political supremacy in the global scenario. 1982 was the summer of the Falklands War. England won the Falklands War against Argentina. They gained supremacy over the world, but there were many shortcomings within England itself. Theroux tries to highlight these shortcomings. As an American, he tries to present the otherness which he sees in England.

In recent travel writings, most travel writers have created the concept of the Other. Theroux being an American views England as the Other in *The Kingdom By The Sea*. Theroux tries to examine the real England beyond the vaunted global superpower. The time of his visit coincides with England's success in the Falklands War where the jubilant Britain managed to prevail over Argentina. However, his tour through Britain brings to light certain contradictions in the condition of people and places which belies its successful image in the world.

Theroux decides to walk around the United Kingdom (Other) and explore how it is different from America (Self). In the travelogue, several descriptions show the comparison or the differences between the two.

Theroux as an outsider seldom had a good word about Britain. He being an American observes England as the other. Although he himself is a Westerner, he looks at Britain or the West as the other.

The Kingdom By The Sea looks at the difference between America and Britain though both are in the Western hemisphere. In this travelogue, a Westerner's view of the West is highlighted, and how he has created the difference among the countries of the West is noticed. Theroux being an American looks at the shortcomings of Britain. Britain's winning of the Falklands War has been criticized here. Although Britain has gained supremacy over the world, there are many shortcomings within the country. Theroux shows Britain as cityless. He has evaluated the English scenario and the problem which troubles the English people.

Paul Theroux's *The Old Patagonian Express: By Train Through The Americas* highlights the concept of the global Other. Beginning his journey in Boston, where he boarded the subway commuter train and caught trains of all kinds on the way, Theroux recounts his journey from ice-bound Massachusetts and Illinois to the arid plateau of Argentina's most southerly trip.

Here he creates the concept of the other world within a train. Given that Theroux is a great believer in train journeys, in the travelogue *The Old Patagonian Express*, the train itself becomes the site for the global scenario. A train is a place where multiple cultures meet.

Theroux need not have to look outside for Othering here; the train itself is a place for Othering. He can see a different world within the train. There are multiple cultures on the train. People from different parts of the world gather, and Theroux while traveling has met different people on the same train.

In the Amtrak's Lake Shore Limited, Theroux met Wendy who was on her way to Ohio, the lady from Flagstaff, a large group of girls heading New Orleans and the Madri Grass, some elderly couple on their way to San Francisco, a couple from Kansas and so on. In The Lone Star, he met a middle-aged couple and a man from Texan, a group of two or three hundred women and children who entered Oklahoma.

The train is a place of multiculturalism. Different people belonging to different cultures are different and based on these differences, Theroux has created the concept of Other in *The Old Patagonian Express*.

Thus, it can be concluded that the Other is an imagined creation of the Self. The Other is based on the hegemonic control of the West over the Orients; the Other is presented as an antithesis to the Self; the Self focuses on the shortcomings of the Other; and the mode of travel can also be a place of Othering. Theroux has created the concept of the Other by observing the people and the places very closely. He has looked at the dressing style, the food habits, the way of talking, as well as the beliefs and practices of the people.

Theroux in his travelogues always presents the Other as fragile, and inferior. He shows the Other as uncivilized, and poor. He extensively criticizes their culture, food habits, dressing styles, their beliefs, and practices. He considers the Self to be superior, and this is more evident in the case of his representation of Oriental countries. The West considers themselves to be superior to the rest of the world.

Theroux from the beginning of the travelogues describes the Other as the worst and shows all the negative aspects of the Other. He provides various instances in his travelogues supporting the Other to be the worst.

Although Theroux criticizes the Other, towards the end he realizes. He repents for the comments he has made towards the Other. He repents the picture which he has presented regarding the Other. Although he presents the Other as inferior, towards the end he tries to show that the Other is not too low or inferior.

CHAPTER TWENTY-FOUR

The Night Train at Deoli-A Story of Love in A Railway Station by Ruskin Bond

Namrata Mukherjee

India is a land of diversity. The beauty of India lies in the fact that it is richly diverse yet magically unified. People living in this country may look, eat, say, or worship in different ways but their hearts are connected as one. In this diversely unique country that we live in, certain things have not, and probably will not, ever, change. These things have left their indelible mark throughout the length and breadth of the country, and all over the country's culture, history, geography, and nostalgia.

One such thing is the railway in India and its trains. They are famous all over the world for bridging the gaps within the country and bringing the North to the South or the East to the West and vice versa. The entire nation of India is connected by the railways and in one way or the other, the train is a part of every single Indian's life.

From the summer vacations when we travelled to our grandma's house by train or while growing up taking different journeys to a lot of different destinations, alone or with others, these journeys have somehow shaped our persona. Trains of India have also been an integral part of various stories penned by different Indian authors. One such storyteller who is also an integral part of the Indian consciousness and has immortalized the train and railways through his tales is none other than Ruskin Bond. We find many instances such as trains, railway stations, tunnels with hidden leopards through which trains will pass, and many more in the rich oeuvre of Mr. Bond's stories. One such beautifully crafted narrative of love, longing, and promises made is his story, "The Night Train at Deoli."

This short but meaningful story has a rich, Indian heart at its core. In the brief span of a few pages, this story can build what many great novels and books cannot, an unforgettable bond. The reader can feel the magic of the story and the strong connection from the heart not just between the narrator, who in this case is the writer himself, and the elusive basket-seller girl but also between themselves and the writer. Bond's extremely powerful wordplay and distinct imagery enable the reader to visualize the story in front of their own eyes. The story has a magical quality like a fairy tale but does not have a typical fairy tale ending. Even then, it is a story for everyone. It is a story of meeting and separation. It is also a story of love and promises, and above all, a story of journey.

The story is simple but special. It is a slice of life of the Indian consciousness and culture portrayed in the guise of a train journey. Bond chooses as his setting an unknown, small-town station hidden in the hills of the Northern Indian terrain which he often crossed during his yearly visits to his grandmother in Dehra. Deoli was only a small town to cross over, just another step in his journey. A name lost in the illustrious crowd of a Delhi or a Dehra, Deoli was a no one. And it is at this no one town's inconspicuous railway station that Bond sets his magical story. But due to his masterful narration, Deoli not only becomes the setting, but a central character who lifts the tale to its magical status. As he says about Deoli, "Why it (the train) stopped at Deoli, I don't know. Nothing ever happened there. Nobody got off the train and nobody got in... I always felt sorry for the lonely little platform and for the place that nobody wanted to visit."

Once on such a visit, when the train stopped at the lonely, Deoli platform, the narrator saw a girl coming up the platform, selling baskets. He was attracted to her dark, eloquent eyes and described her as "She was a young girl walking with dignity. Her feet were bare and her clothes were old." Both of them looked at each other for a long time, and he felt as if her eyes were searching for something. The girl asked him to buy a basket and just as he took one the train jolted out of its stupor and started moving out of the platform. The train left, taking the narrator along but he was not able to forget the girl, especially her eyes. "I sat awake for the rest of the journey. I could not rid my mind of the picture of the girl's face and her smouldering eyes."

Although her memory faded in the spiral of activities and life at Dehra, on the return journey the author remembered her and longed to see her. The girl returned his familiarity and longing when the train reached Deoli. They both smiled when they saw each other. It was like two old friends meeting after a long time, and each was happy to be remembered by the other. It was as if the lonely friendless station and platform at Deoli had given these two people their connection in the universe, their little world of love. Even if they did not speak, they were eloquent, an eloquence that went beyond words. The narrator wanted to take the girl away with him, on the train but left her with a promise of coming back. He had to go to Delhi but the girl had nowhere to go. He promised to come back and she promised to be there for him.

This time when the narrator left Deoli, the girl was there with him as a bright, loving memory. She was with him, always. He couldn't wait to get back and find her, and bring her away with him. On his next visit, as the train drew into Deoli, he was excited and nervous at the thought of seeing her again. But fate her other plans. She was not there waiting, to go away with him. He searched up and down the platform and asked around but the girl was not there. Broken-hearted, the narrator shortened his stay at Dehra and took the train back to the plains. On his return journey, the tea seller at the tea stall of Deoli remembered the girl but was not able to say anything about what happened to her. He did not need to because she was nothing to him. The brief, loving encounter of the narrator had become a memory. It was a dream that stayed with him forever. He wanted to take the girl away, for the sense of responsibility and tenderness that he felt for her were always there, except for the girl herself.

A nameless station that no one visited or loved, left the narrator with one of the brightest longings of his life. There were two promises made in the story and somehow none were kept. The girl promised to be there for him and he promised to take her away, but the star-crossed lovers lost each other on the Deoli platform. The narrator had also made a promise to the town of Deoli to break his journey and spend some time there. But out of his longing for the girl, he was not able to keep that as well. He let her live in his heart, in his memories, with the not-so-sure hope of seeing her again, someday. He could not bring himself to go into Deoli and find out what happened to her, but rather, let her be a mystery, probably a piece of fiction, and never allowed himself to come out of this reverie.

Thus, he ends the story by saying, "In the last few years I have passed through Deoli many times, and I always look out of the carriage window, half expecting to see the same unchanged face smiling up at me. I wonder what happens in Deoli, behind the station walls. But I will never break my journey there. It may spoil my game. I prefer to keep hoping and dreaming, and looking out of the window up and down that lonely platform, waiting for the girl with the baskets. I never break my journey at Deoli, but I pass through as often as I can.

CHAPTER TWENTY-FIVE

My Memories on the Train

K.Venkata Lakshmi

Train journeys are more economical, comfortable and enjoyable. I have had innumerable memories when I used to travel with my three-year-old kid. Those memories are unforgettable and filled with enthusiasm. I started my first journey to Delhi with my 3-year-old kid on September 11th in 2011 along with my husband. That was the first time I had encountered so many landscapes and different cultures. I was astonished while we were crossing Agra on hearing about the Taj Mahal. I used to travel every year from Delhi to Hyderabad without my husband's presence. Generally, we used to start on May 16th and return in the last week of June to Delhi.

Every time I boarded the train with two bags. My bags were stuffed with rotis and my son's Summer homework. I made my child complete his one and half month homework in one and half days during the train journey. I was immensely feared when I left my child with others while going to restrooms. I had spent all the five years in Delhi in a similar manner. I still cherish the memory of the vendor selling bread omelets with my son who pronounced it as 'blood omelet' and wanted it even after my rebukes. Those days are long gone.

After that I have never opted for train journeys as we have settled in Hyderabad. Now my son is a teenager and when I tell him these incidents to him he says 'po amma'. Finally, I want to sum those golden days as unforgettable and everlasting memories during the course of my life.

CHAPTER TWENTY-SIX

Inside a Magnificent Box!

Disha Shetty

Sitting on sand, sipping my caramelized salted mocha (just tea at beach) I wrote down in my notebook. Get work, get money, get respect etc etc...until I realized I forgot to mention to get myself.

City of dreams it is no doubt and like every other dreamer I go from east to west holding a bar right above my head.

Everytime I am inside the magnificent box (referring to the local trains of Mumbai)I only speak to myself one day no more holding the bar, no more get work, get money , get respect , get blah blah blah...it will only be go get your life before it's too late.

My caramelized mocha almost got cold when a huge wave hit by the shore and I was quiet busy adoring a four leg animal right in front of my door.

How lucky was he playing in the sand without a thing to regret. Me so damn jealous so just laid my hands back a little bit in order to stretch, until I realized people simply gazed at me wondering how lovely her life is, enjoying her own company.

Just so humane I thought to have somebody so close to chits and bhelpuri chats.

No wonder that mocha tastes so bitter so shit it was all a mishap indeed,

But there's no way out other than from West to east again not holding the bar this but feeling my legs all a wide,

And yet
I like how peaceful and glamourous this Magnificent Box seems
at the stroke of twilight...!

To the Busy Days Dread

Kavya Dinesh

Melodious welcome as we embarked
On the train with passengers enlaced.
In the cooling domain, aides on board
Brought the serving board
With newspapers and snacks prepaid
In an opulent parade.

Adding to the comfort, the hot coffees' warmth
Emerged the best in the raining forth.
Gently washing the panes, the droplets
Mirrored the musings of those immersed in gadgets
Chumming with the notes of their musical hooks.

And thus, the ease endured...
The joy of the journey ensured.

But soon the train slowed its pace
As the rain sped its race.
Debris filled the tracks
Our faces hit with smacks
Of unrest for the delay,
Struggling to curb our dismay.

Fidgeting in seats,
We upended the bites,
Stuck amidst on the workers in rag, our wandering gaze,
Acting on the tracks to clear our ways,
Galloping in a blink to the happy waving kids
Cladded in tatters, to the travellers vexed.

We flew for a moment with carefree wings
In their welkin of lovely springs
For the truth flashed before us that
Though upon this noble perch they may never chat,
The beauty of life lies
In the modesty of these unhurried lives.
    Once again, we leapt ahead
To the busy days dread
With the train moving away
From the children's play.

CHAPTER TWENTY-EIGHT

The Train as an Archetype as Seen in Classic Malayalam Movies

Neenu Kuruvilla

The long rail paths, sometimes glittering in the burning sun, at times soaked in heavy downpour, sometimes frozen in winter chill, sometimes laden with beauty of spring with overshadowing willow trees, often adopt seasonal charms attuned with seasons and its cycles. A train could become a metaphor for human psyche acting as a significant metaphor for highly turbulent or complicated human subconscious. The paper makes an attempt to derive a new literary archetype to denote human psyche -the train and its metaphorical resemblance with human psyche.

The classical Malayalam movies cleverly inculcated into it an imagery of train-either at the beginning or at its crisis or at its all resolving climax. Some of them reserved the train element to the rear end to denote a perfect resolution for the movie line. But this seemly resolution making imagery of train leaves the movies open ended providing with the central characters a fresh aspect of his/ her psyche.

Thoovanathumbikal, the most celebrated Padma Rajan movie which broke all the conventional norms of familial system and quintessential attributes befitting a hero, portrayed a hero who had a multiple sort of identity. Portraying a rural, naïve, filthy farmer on the one side and projecting a very contrary city bred man on the other end, the hero seems to be complicated in himself. As suggested by Freud in his theory of id, ego and super ego, the city bred man in the movie fells for Clara – an outcaste, prostitute who always appears as a mythical figure with the accompaniment of rain. The other half of the hero's identity falls for Radha who belongs to the same caste and religion, a well-mannered, educated girl.

The hero faces severe existential crisis, torn himself between Radha and Clara, unable to make a decision as to whom his identity should embrace. One half craves for Clara, a very passionate, emotional crave highly supported by the irrationality of heart. The other half voluntarily decides to enter into institution of marriage with Radha, a decision taken by the rationality and logical thinking part of the brain. There is a heart - brain conflict which could not reach at a resolution and the entry of a long-distance train at archetypal looking Ottapalam station brings a resolution to hero's mind.

The climax scene is noteworthy for its depiction of a railway station and entry of a train. Clara steps down from the train embellished herself in a silk saree, with neatly tied hair almost making her fit for an institution like familial arena. The hero then comes to know that Clara is now married to a wealthy business man. The meeting at railway station with Clara, her husband and their new born, forces the hero to boldly arrive at a resolution that Clara is gone for ever and now Radha is there for him. The passing train in the back ground, symbolized the passing memory of Clara and a new union with Radha.

The train element here act as an archetype of individuation and identity formation of an individual. The hero heavily trapped in existential crisis, never knew where to place himself. Suspended in the intricacies of life he vainly searches for meaning of life in seemly mundane things. But never was he able to arrive at a resolution or identity formation. A primitive, naïve, raw side of him urged for most instinctual, biological, nature given urge of associating himself with Clara who always came with warmth of nature, i.e. rain. Life then got itself attuned with the rhythm of the nature, the sound of the beach, biological instinctual urge to mate, rain which poured transcending time and place, unending chats about meaning of life and love, seemingly heathen or pagan return to primordial existence. Hero was thrown almost into a trance feeling, an unusual transcendental relationship with Clara which is not earthy or mundane. The seemingly unconventional relationship helps the hero to break every societal norm and embrace an ultimate bliss almost similar to Carnivalism propounded by Bakhtin.

On the other end, Radha, as the name itself suggests, a virgin girl of same caste, sister to his acquaintance, a very distant relative, tied closely in religious ceremonies, often meeting in family gathering, rituals and temples, Radha becomes someone who could easily fit into traditional familial status of hero. She becomes the epitome of a system or to put it theoretically an icon of ideological state apparatus who governs the institutionalised man in the hero. The hero attains an individuation or gets converted into an ego with due intervention of Radha. Marriage on onside which is highly legalized and extra marital affair on the other end which is highly illegal and immoral, attaining an identity becomes a trauma which the hero faces.

The perfect resolution is achieved at the climax stage when a long-distance train enters into the frame bringing out solutions and consolations. The train imagery brings with it a married Clara which literally meant she no more belongs to the hero and reinforces the power of institutionalized ritual of marriage. The passing train and the Ottapalam station with hinges of tender wave and rhythm of slow-moving train, becomes an ionic representation of the hero reassuring his ego as an institutionalised human.

Yet another classic movie *Nakashathagal* directed by Hariharan and written by M.T Vasudevan Nair brings into it a rushing train towards its climax to depict a perfect ending for the movie. Hero torn between love for a simple village girl and a promised marriage with his employer's dump daughter, unable to take a decision, puts an end to his life by throwing himself to the rushing wheels of a furious moving train. The train here becomes an archetype or a metaphor which untangled the hero from the dilemma that he was facing. An assured high-status life on one side with promised wealth, status, fame and popularity the hero still craves for the raw and naïve affection he felt for the simple village girl. Caught between the binaries and unable to arrive a perfect resolution, he decided to put an end to his life where train act as yet another archetype.

Neelavelicham by Basheer depicts a train sequence which brings the crisis part of the movie. The train witness a murder in cold blood done by the villain to procure the love of his life. The heroine who come to know about the incident commits suicide and gets transformed herself into the form of a **Yakshi** who then cleverly intervene with yet another person's life to unveil the mystery behind her lover's death. The train sequence acts as a proper interlude to bring transformation to life of heroine, hence forth attaining a more transcendental stance.

The three movie **Thoovanathumbikal ,Nagashathagal,Neelavelicham** use train element at its climax or crisis stage and plays a pivotal role in the life of characters. The characters hence forth try to bring a resolution to their life dilemmas by relying heavily upon the train elements. If the hero embraced the conventional part of the identity after the entry of the train in climax of **Thoovanathumbikal.** the hero found a solution to his crisis by depending on train element in **Nagashatagal.** The heroine decides to take a transcendental stance after coming to know the murder in the train as seen in **Neelavelicham.** Train too could at times act as an archetype that transcend time and place and could bring a perfect answer to never ending quest of life-self-knowledge.

CHAPTER TWENTY-NINE

Trains as Symbols of Connection and Separation During the Partition of India and Pakistan

Preeti Sharma

The Partition of India and Pakistan in 1947 is one of the most traumatic events in the history of the subcontinent. This period was marked by the mass migration of millions, intense communal violence, and lasting emotional scars. Central to this upheaval were trains, which became powerful symbols of both connection and separation. These iron giants, crisscrossing the newly drawn borders, embodied the dual nature of human relationships during this chaotic time—binding people together while simultaneously tearing them apart.

CONNECTION: UNITING LIVES AMIDST TURMOIL

Before Partition, trains were symbols of the unity of the Indian subcontinent. They linked distant cities, facilitated trade, and brought together people from various cultures. Railway stations were vibrant microcosms of Indian society, bustling with people from different backgrounds. Trains represented the shared history and collective identity of the subcontinent's diverse population.

However, during the Partition, the role of trains changed dramatically. They became lifelines for millions of refugees fleeing communal violence. For many, boarding these trains was an act of hope and survival, the only way to traverse vast distances to the newly designated nations of India and Pakistan. The carriages, packed beyond capacity, became places where stories of loss and resilience were exchanged, creating temporary communities united by a common destiny.

Despite the pervasive fear and uncertainty, trains also facilitated poignant moments of human connection. Families and friends, separated by the new borders, used the railway system to send letters and messages, maintaining a fragile thread of communication. For many, the train journeys during this period were filled with memories of farewells and reunions, encapsulating the paradox of connection amidst separation.

SEPARATION: THE AGONY OF PARTING

While trains served as lifelines, they also became grim symbols of separation. The same tracks that once united people now carried them to different, often hostile lands. Stations that were once filled with the excitement of travel became scenes of heart-wrenching goodbyes. Families watched helplessly as loved ones boarded trains to uncertain futures, knowing they might never meet again.

The violence of Partition also stained the legacy of trains. There are harrowing accounts of trains arriving at stations filled not with hopeful passengers but with the bodies of those who had been killed in route. These "ghost trains" became horrifying symbols of the brutality and sectarian hatred that accompanied the subcontinent's division. The railway tracks, which once symbolized connection, now stood as stark reminders of the severance and sorrow inflicted by Partition.

Trains also symbolized the forced migration and dislocation experienced by millions. People were uprooted from their ancestral homes, their identities reshaped by the political upheaval. The trains carried not just individuals, but entire cultures and histories, now disjointed and scattered across new borders. The journey for many was a passage from a known past into an uncertain future, amplifying the sense of loss and separation.

STORY OF RAVI AND AYESHA

Ravi and Ayesha, childhood friends, grew up in a village near the railway tracks. Their friendship was as steadfast as the iron rails that stretched across the land. They spent countless afternoons playing by the station, their laughter mingling with the distant rumble of approaching trains. But with Partition, the trains took on a new significance. Ravi, a Hindu, and Ayesha, a Muslim, found themselves on opposite sides of a newly drawn border that neither understood nor accepted.

One evening, as the sun set and cast long shadows over the station, Ravi and Ayesha met by the tracks. The air was heavy with fear and the smell of burning homes. Ravi held a tattered photograph of his family, while Ayesha clutched a small silver locket, a gift from her grandmother.

"We're leaving tomorrow," Ravi whispered. "The train to Delhi."

Ayesha's eyes filled with tears. "We're going to Lahore. My father says we have no choice."

They sat in silence, the reality of their separation sinking in. The train that had always symbolized their shared adventures was now a harbinger of their parting. The next morning, the station was chaotic. Families huddled together, clutching their belongings, eyes wide with fear and uncertainty. Ravi's family waited for the train to Delhi. Across the station, Ayesha's family prepared for the train to Lahore. As the Delhi-bound train approached, Ravi spotted Ayesha. He broke away from his family and ran to her, weaving through the throngs of people. When he reached her, he pressed the photograph into her hand.

"Keep this," he said. "So, you'll remember."

Ayesha, her eyes brimming with tears, handed him the silver locket. "And you, this. So, you'll never forget."

The train to Delhi arrived with a cacophony of screeching brakes and shouts. Ravi's family hurried him on board, and he watched as Ayesha's form grew smaller and smaller until she was just a speck on the horizon. The train lurched forward, carrying him away from everything he had known. As the train sped through the countryside, Ravi held the locket tightly, the cool metal a stark contrast to the heat of his hand. He could feel the distance growing between him and Ayesha, each mile a painful reminder of their separation. Yet, amidst the despair, the locket was a beacon of their enduring connection.

On the other side, Ayesha boarded the train to Lahore, clutching the photograph. As the train rattled along the tracks, she traced the faces in the picture, her heart aching with loss. The photograph was a link to Ravi, a promise that their bond would transcend the new borders drawn by men.

Years passed, and both Ravi and Ayesha built new lives in their respective countries. The trains that had once symbolized their connection and separation became memories etched in their hearts. They never saw each other again, but they held onto the tokens of their friendship, reminders of a time before the world were torn apart.

In the twilight of their lives, Ravi and Ayesha would sometimes sit by the tracks, in their respective lands, listening to the distant rumble of trains. And in those moments, they felt a connection that no border could erase, a silent testimony to the enduring power of human bonds amidst the forces of separation.

THE DUALITY OF TRAINS

The dual symbolism of trains during the Partition of India and Pakistan reflects the complexities of human experiences during times of upheaval. Trains served as lifelines for refugees, bridging the gap between their past homes and uncertain futures. They became moving sanctuaries where strangers shared their fears and hopes, forming transient communities bound by the shared experience of displacement. The very act of boarding a train was a leap of faith, a desperate bid for survival and a new beginning.

Yet, the same trains also carried the weight of separation and loss. They ferried individuals away from their ancestral lands, tearing families apart and scattering communities across the subcontinent. Each journey was fraught with peril, as trains that once symbolized progress and connection were now seen as routes of escape or corridors of death. The term "ghost trains" evokes the haunting reality of carriages arriving at stations filled not with survivors but with the remnants of massacres, their silence more deafening than the roar of their engines.

Moreover, trains symbolized the irreversible changes wrought by Partition. They transported not just people but entire ways of life, cultural traditions, and personal histories. Every station stop marked a departure from the familiar, embedding the physical and emotional distance into the passengers' hearts. The relentless motion of the trains mirrored the unstoppable tide of change sweeping the land, transforming it beyond recognition.

This duality is what makes the imagery of trains during Partition so compelling and poignant. On one hand, they represented the enduring human spirit, the ability to connect and find solidarity in the face of adversity. On the other hand, they were a stark reminder of the arbitrary and violent severing of bonds, the finality of departures, and the irrevocable alteration of lives.

In modern narratives, stories of Partition trains evoke both the tragedy of separation and the resilience of human connections. Films, literature, and oral histories often revisit these journeys, emphasizing how, despite physical divisions, the shared human spirit endured. The legacy of these trains is a testament to the enduring bonds that transcend political boundaries, highlighting the paradoxical nature of connection amidst separation.

CONCLUSION

The trains of Partition are enduring symbols of one of the most significant events in South Asian history. They encapsulate the essence of connection and separation, illustrating how human relationships were both forged and fractured during this period. As lifelines of hope and harbingers of sorrow, these trains remain etched in collective memory, reminding us of the profound impact of Partition on the lives of millions. The legacy of these trains continues to resonate, a powerful testament to the enduring strength of human connections amidst the forces of separation. In the sweltering heat of August 1947, the village of Amritpur lay under a canopy of uncertainty. The Partition of India and Pakistan was not just a political event; it was a seismic shift that would reshape millions of lives. The railway station, usually a bustling hub of activity, now stood as a silent witness to the unfolding drama of connection and separation.

CHAPTER THIRTY

Being a Rail Fan in India

Vastav Shastri

In India, we refer to those who are passionate about trains as "rail fans." This pastime or passion of watching trains and gathering information about trains, locomotives, coaches, and wagons (yep!) is quite difficult to put into words. Yes, you read that correctly; we do gather information on the locopilots of the specific trains and freight wagons. When someone inquires about my pastime or my passion, I explain my activity in a very straightforward manner, saying that as many people as possible are interested in automobiles, sports vehicles, sports bikes, airplanes, and so on. I am quite enthusiastic about trains. When I see trains, I can't help but take pictures of them. This causes a lot of people to laugh out loud. What could possibly cause someone to become so enraged by trains? People in other nations, like the United Kingdom and the United States, widely recognize the existence of a sizable community of rail enthusiasts. The information that they share pertains to trains as well as many features of railways, including signaling, tracks, and other technical aspects. A fact that may come as a surprise to readers is that we do, in fact, celebrate the birthday of trains every year. We hold a cake-cutting ceremony on the occasion of the birthday, referring to the inauguration date of that specific train. On days like this, railfans participate in decorating the locomotive and cutting the cake with members of the crew. The authorities in charge of railways have previously authorized all these activities. The birthday celebration of the 12951/12952 Mumbai Rajdhani Express, which runs daily between Mumbai Central and New Delhi, takes place on May 17th of each year. This is one of the few times that it takes place. Railroad enthusiasts from a variety of cities travel to Mumbai in order to take part in this event, and they typically board this train back to their respective cities.

Trains have captivated me since I was a child in the late 1990s. My father was a college professor at the time, so the institution assigned us a residential quarter on its campus. Our home, which we had resided in for twenty years, was a two-story structure. We gave the ground floor to the college's English professor, Dr. Sanadhya, and the first floor to ourselves. Dr. Sanadhya's younger brother lived in a separate location; he and his family used to visit only on Sundays and holidays. Every Sunday, Dr. Sanadhya's nephew would visit the house. Amardeep and I are in the same age group. I used to spend the entire week, from Monday to Saturday, playing and romping alone on campus in the evenings. During those days, Sundays and other holidays held a special significance for me, as they provided me with the rare opportunity to play with someone my own age. On days like these, I would become frustrated when he failed to show up, forcing me to confront my feelings of isolation once more. It is clear that my grandfather has a good understanding of the situation I was in. The first time I ever encountered a train was when he took me on a ride in a double-decker bus that began at the college campus, traveled to the railway station, and then returned to the campus. My grandfather and I used to spend an hour or two at the station. This was my first experience with trains. In my city of Surat, there are no longer any double-decker buses operating.

Those of us who are aficionados of trains have never referred to a train by its name; instead, we only recall the numbers of the trains. Take, for instance, the Flying Ranee Express (12921/12922), the Karnvati Express (12933/12934), and their respective numbers. We can learn about the specific details of the train by paying attention to the minute details of the coach. For example, if we notice the printed number on the coach, it can provide us with information about the year the coach was manufactured (for example, if the coach number is 04052, the first two digits of the number suggest that it was built in 2004). The signalling system is where the most intriguing aspects of trains can be found. One yellow signal denotes caution, which means proceed and be prepared to stop at the next signal; two yellow signals suggest proceed and be prepared to pass the next signal at such speed indicated in the order; and a green signal shows the authorization to proceed further. The red signal indicates that the train should come to a complete stop.

We used to visit Mumbai during summer vacations only that to for a day or two, as we couldn't bear to leave my grandfather home all day alone. The approximately 265 kilometres between Surat and Mumbai used to take trains four or five hours to cover. So far, the duration has been cut to three hours. In the '90s, our favourite train was the Karnavati Express (Ahmedabad to Mumbai Central), which used to depart from Surat at about 8:00 a.m. and arrive in Mumbai at about 12:30 p.m. Like many kids on planes, I used to jump up into the window seat whenever we went on a journey. While traveling with my family, I overheard my dad telling my mom, "now he (me) will forget us for three to four hours..." each time, and I couldn't help but smile quietly to myself. Notable among the travellers were Cutlet and Poha. The Pantry Car odf this train still serves the most delicious and fresh cutlet. Most families usually bring thepla, khakhara, and fafda (Gujarati Snacks) along, which are home-cooked meals. Unlike me, my dad has strong opinions on this matter. He always brings this up: we should give vendors a chance to make money whenever we go out, not only on train excursions! There was a time when this made us giggle. Aside from his humorous side, my dad is a serious foodie. He really didn't want my mom to have to deal with the stress of making breakfast first thing in the morning. I used to bring a notebook and pen with me on train trips so that I could remember the names of the stations and when our train would stop at each one.

It is conceivable that I may assert that this served as the basis on which my hobby was built. The location of my aunt's home was in the suburban area of Mumbai known as Malad. Currently, my aunt's entire family has relocated to the United States. They resided in the Meena Apartment, which was located in close proximity to the Railway Level Crossing. My uncle used to take my cousin Amee and me to the railway cabin, which was located near the railway level crossing. This train cabin is currently being dismantled by the railways so that new lines can be installed. Counting the number of local trains that went up and down (Virar to Churchgate) was something we used to do with great precision. In those days, we tried to mimic the sound of the wheels gliding over the rail joints. We wouldn't go back up the Railway Level until the two diesel-powered trains, the August Kranti Rajdhani Express and the Mumbai Rajdhani, had passed. This scene remains vivid in my memory, and it brings me great delight to witness it. It encompasses the resounding noise of diesel engines, the humming of power-generating coach, and the captivating combination of red and cream paint on the train. This sight is still extremely vivid in my mind, and it remains a joy to behold. I cannot express how delighted I am to be able to view it. There were occasions when we went out to the terrace of that flat to watch trains, particularly the Rajdhani Express, which was regarded as the most prestigious and quickest train of those days. It was a visual feast to witness Mumbai local trains and mail or express trains racing together. In fact, it is a sight to behold. Traveling via Rajdhani Express was like a dream for me. When I was little, I asked my father why we always took the Kutch Express back to Surat and never the Rajdhani Express. While maintaining his composure, my father stated that the ticket for this train is rather expensive and that we are unable to purchase it. I was really upset when I heard this from my father, and I told my mother about it. It used to bring tears to my eyes when my mother told me that when I grew up and started earning money, I'd be able to take this train. She said it with all the warmth and charm she could manage.

When I was in sixth grade, the teacher asked the entire class, "What do you envision yourself doing in the future?" All of the kids began to react one by one; some wanted to be physicians, others wanted to be engineers, and yet others wanted to be business owners. My roll number, 61, was the second-last in the class. This was because roll numbers were assigned alphabetically based on the surname. Even if they had issued roll numbers based on my name or my father's name, I would have remained in the same position. My father's name starts with the letter 'V,' while my surname starts with 'S........ As soon as it was my turn, I announced that I wanted to work as an engine driver on a train (at the time, I was unfamiliar with the term "locopilot"), and everyone laughed at me because it was not a job that was considered mainstream or anticipated by others. Despite this, most people are unfamiliar with rail vocabulary, which includes terms like locomotive, rake, locomotive's class, and shed, among others. For example, if the letter ERS appears in front of the locomotive next to the locomotive number, it means that the locomotive is owned by the Ernakulam shed, where it undergoes primary maintenance. On the other hand, if the letter WAP 7 is inscribed on the locomotive, it can be deciphered as W for wide gauge, A for electric traction, P for passenger train, etc. India is home to a big number of railfans who are not just passionate about trains but have also built a career out of writing books about them. One of the books to consider is "Halt Station India: The Dramatic Tale of the Nation's First Rail Lines" by Rajendra B. Aklekar.

During my time in college, I discovered IRFCA.org, a website dedicated to railfans. The term IRFCA refers to the Indian Railways Fan Club Association. This is the name of a website made by Indian railfans. The photographs of Indian railways included on this website are among the most exclusive ever captured by railfans from all around India. This website also includes information about locomotives, sheds, and technical specs for the locomotives listed. Surat, the city where I live, is home to approximately fifteen railfans. It is traditional for us to converge at the station on notable occasions, like as the Rajdhani Express's birthday, which falls on May 17th each year, to see the famous train. On the 50th anniversary of the Mumbai Rajdhani Express, a group of Mumbai railfans took the train from Mumbai to Delhi. En-route, they celebrated this train's birthday with the train's manager and workers. Others may find it odd, but the railfan community will remember it for a long time.

Other passengers consider the honking of a locomotive and the sound produced as the wheels cross from track junctions to be noise, while railfans regard it as nothing short of pure ecstasy. Over the course of the past ten years, the authorities in charge of railways have begun to acknowledge the passion of railfans and to appreciate the efforts that railroad enthusiasts put forth. Railways frequently include photographs and videos taken by railfans on their social media pages, along with credit information for the photographers and videographers. It is impossible to adequately convey the endless affection for love that is pulsating in the center of each and every railfan through the use of words.

CHAPTER THIRTY-ONE

Mysteries and Adventures on the Rails

Inderjot Kaur

Railways have long captivated the imagination of adventurers and storytellers alike, serving as the backdrop for tales of intrigue, suspense, and discovery. The rhythmic clack of the tracks, the haunting whistle of the locomotive, and the vast landscapes rolling by have all contributed to the allure of train travel. In this essay, we delve into the world of mysteries and adventures on the rails, exploring the rich tapestry of stories that have unfolded within the confines of train carriages.

Train travel has always held a special place in the hearts of travelers, evoking a sense of nostalgia and romance. From the opulent luxury of the Orient Express to the rugged charm of the Trans-Siberian Railway, trains have been synonymous with adventure and exploration. The allure of distant destinations and the promise of new experiences have drawn countless individuals to embark on journeys across continents, forging connections and creating memories along the way.

One of the most compelling aspects of train travel is the potential for mysterious encounters. The confined space of a train carriage creates a microcosm of society, where strangers are thrust together for hours or even days at a time. Within this confined space, secrets are whispered, alliances are formed, and unexpected connections are made. From chance encounters with enigmatic strangers to the discovery of hidden compartments and clandestine activities, trains provide the perfect setting for mysteries to unfold.

The golden age of rail travel, spanning the late 19th and early 20th centuries, was a time of unprecedented luxury and elegance. From lavish dining cars to sumptuous sleeping compartments, trains of this era offered unparalleled comfort and style. It was also a time of great social upheaval and political intrigue, with spies, diplomats, and adventurers crisscrossing the globe in pursuit of their objectives. The romance and glamour of this bygone era have inspired countless works of fiction, from classic detective stories to sweeping historical dramas.

Some train journeys have achieved legendary status, their names synonymous with adventure and exploration. The Trans-Siberian Railway, stretching over 9,000 kilometers from Moscow to Vladivostok, is the longest continuous railway line in the world, traversing vast expanses of wilderness and connecting diverse cultures and landscapes. The Indian Pacific, crossing the Australian continent from Sydney to Perth, offers a journey through the heart of the outback, with stunning desert vistas and rugged mountain ranges. These iconic journeys have inspired writers, filmmakers, and travelers alike, capturing the imagination with their promise of adventure and discovery.

Alongside the romance and adventure, train travel has also been the backdrop for a host of unsolved mysteries and unexplained phenomena. From disappearances and murders to ghostly apparitions and paranormal encounters, trains have been at the center of countless tales of the unknown. The eerie sound of phantom footsteps echoing through deserted carriages, the sight of shadowy figures lurking in the darkness, and the feeling of unease that pervades deserted stations at night—all contribute to the sense of mystery and intrigue that surrounds train travel.

In conclusion, mysteries and adventures on the rails have captured the imagination of generations of travelers and storytellers. From the romance and glamour of the golden age of rail travel to the intrigue and suspense of mysterious encounters, trains have provided the perfect setting for tales of adventure and discovery. Whether traversing vast continents or exploring remote wilderness, the allure of train travel continues to captivate and inspire, promising endless possibilities for those bold enough to embark on the journey.

CHAPTER THIRTY-TWO

Tracks of Destiny

Aardra H

On the tracks of destiny, the journey began..
Passengers abroad, each with a tale
Of triumph & struggle, of heaven & hell;
Bound for destinations, both near & far
Among them sat a girl, lost in thought..
Whispers of memories, haunting & cold
In the depths of despair, the story unfolds
Through the maze of sorrow, she wanders alone
Seeking solace from a life unmarked
Though the road is long and the way unsure..
Through the clatter of wheels & the whistle's cry
As landscape shifted,
She found the courage to embrace a new life.
For on this train, amidst the journey's strife..
She left behind the burdens &
Discovered the essence of life.
In the tapestry of life,
For even in darkness, there's a thread of grace..
Let the whistle blow,
Let the tracks stretch out,
Let the journey unfold..
For every journey has lessons to learn,

And she found the strength to
Soar wide.....

www.ingramcontent.com/pod-product-compliance
Lightning Source LLC
Chambersburg PA
CBHW031145130726
47988CB00006B/2546